THE SCOUNDREL'S CHRISTMAS CHALLENGE

ONCE UPON A WIDOW 9 WICKED WIDOWS LEAGUE 27

AUBREY WYNNE

ISBN:978-1-946560-34-6

Editing by The Editing Hall

Cover Art by Mandy Koehler Design

❀ Created with Vellum

SERIES LIST

Keep updated on future releases, exclusive excerpts, and prizes by following my newsletter:
https://www.subscribepage.com/k3f1z5

Once Upon a Widow series (sweet Regency)
Earl of Sunderland #1
A Wicked Earl's Widow #2
Rhapsody and Rebellion #3
Earl of Darby #4
Earl of Brecken #5
Earl of Griffith #6
Beware a Wallflower's Wrath #7
A Wallflower's Wassail Punch #8
The Scoundrel's Christmas Challenge #9
The Duplicate Duke #10

Read on Kindle Unlimited
A MacNaughton Castle Romance (steamy Regency Highland series)

A Merry MacNaughton Mishap (Prequel) (only sweet romance in series)

Deception and Desire #1

Allusive Love #2

A Bonny Pretender #3

This story is for anyone who enjoys good banter, roots for unrequited love, and adores Christmas romance. I hope this story leaves my readers with a smile and eager to enjoy the holidays.

PRAISE FOR ONCE UPON A WIDOW SERIES

Praise for Once Upon a Widow series

"Historically accurate with poignant characters dealing with strife so gut-wrenching, I can't even imagine how I'd respond. Gripping story with an explosive ending."

N.N. Light Book Heaven Reviews

"Aubrey Wynne's epic historical romance bedazzles as much as it leaves the reader breathless! Her intricate details lavish the reader with picturesque landscapes, scrumptious dialogue, leaving nothing too small to define."

InD'tale Magazine

"Somewhere between Austin and Heyer. A good read."

Verified Purchase review

"The scenes are so graphically detailed and descriptive, it paints an elegant backdrop that makes the storyline pop."

Verified Purchase Reviewer

"Aubrey wields her words as skillfully and precise as a surgeon with his scalpel."

Verifed Purchase Reviewer

"I highly recommend."

Jersey Girl Book Lover

SUMMARY

A contest to win her fortune...

Lady Winfield, a wealthy widow of six years, is infamous for her outrageous house parties. While hosting her annual Christmastide gathering, Christiana proposes a new game: a daily challenge of her choice. She will accept the proposal of the man who can best her at three or more competitions by Twelfth Night. Though all agree to the diversion, no one expects the games to include marksmanship, archery, and fencing.

A contest to win her heart...

Lucius, Viscount Page has held a torch for the countess since his university days. But he doused the flames of passion after she married his best friend. Ten years later, the embers begin a slow burn when he learns Christiana may be ready for another husband. Lucius, determined not to waste this second chance at love, presents the audacious Lady Winfield with a secret challenge that she can't resist.

Will their midnight rendezvous and private contests end in certain victory for one or a dual attraction for both?

PROLOGUE

June 1815
Almack's London

ucius, Viscount Page raked his gaze across the ballroom filled with the Season's latest hopefuls. His sister, Annette, was busy with a group of attendees, so he took the opportunity to move toward the exit. Just as he reached the door, he glanced over his shoulder and saw Nettie waving at him furiously, pushing through the crowd to reach him.

Blast! He tossed her a wicked smile and slid from the room, pulling out his flask at the same time the oak door slammed shut behind him. Taking the stairs to the next level below, he found a dark dusty alcove and settled in for a strong drink. But the whisky did nothing to banish the memories assailing him this evening. Lucius had managed not to think of her for an entire week and then... *Smack!* Her smiling face had returned, taunting, laughing, alluring.

It had been the chit in the pale-rose silk with the honey-blonde hair. The tiny glass birds dangling from her ears as if trying to take flight, the wings glittering with the woman's every step. She'd looked like Christiana's twin from the back. *Nodcock!* Was that all it took for her to saturate his thoughts again? He tipped the flask and took a long draw, then smacked his lips and let out a defeated sigh.

"Lucius, you shouldn't have," Christiana exclaimed, her light-blue eyes sparkling as she removed the delicate crystal figurine from the velvet. She held it up, watching the hand-painted swan shimmer beneath the candlelight.

"You told me they represent grace. Something you have in spades." Lucius smiled, feeling ridiculously pleased with himself. The gift had set him back a bit, eating up half his allowance for the month. The delight in Tia's eyes was worth it.

"And fidelity," she added, casting him a sly look from beneath dark-blonde lashes. "When do you leave for university? I shall miss you, Lord Page."

"Not until after Epiphany. You won't get rid of me so quickly."

"You will leave, make new friends, and forget about me."

She was such a beauty, even when she pouted. "Never," he said and meant it.

Lucius took another pull from his flask. He shouldn't have left Nettie alone, but he planned on returning before the doors were locked at eleven. After which, not even a duke could cross the threshold. No one would bother his sister, he thought with confidence, not with four protective brothers watching over her.

Footsteps echoed in the stairwell, growing louder. Lucius leaned farther into the alcove, his dark coat blending into the shadows. When the figure emerged onto the landing, he smiled to himself. Nettie always had been like a bloodhound when it came to her siblings. She could sniff them out from any hiding place.

Silent, he watched as Nettie poked her head around the corner, looking up the next flight. With a sigh, she turned on her heel. Lucius smiled.

"You smell of whisky."

Devil it! His smile faded. "Good whisky. Expensive whisky," answered Lucius. "Less of a headache tomorrow."

"Brother, why do you torture yourself so?" Lady Annette Page, standing with her hands on her slender hips, the paste emeralds in her dark hair catching the weak light from the wall sconce, was a force to be reckoned with. Irritation flashed in her green eyes, so like his own, almost matching the Pomona silk of her dress. Annette knew of the Christiana tragedy, but Lucius would never admit to being lovesick.

She sighed. "I miss her too. She taught me all the ridiculous, intricate rules I needed for my first Season. Not that I remember them all. I so wish she was here to help me through it."

A low growl started in Lucius's throat. He'd met the honied-hair beauty at a Christmas ball, where she'd stolen his heart. They had written while he was at university, and he had plans to marry her when he finished. But when he came home with best friend and ever-charming rogue, the Earl of Winfield in tow, the scoundrel had wooed her himself.

Proposed.

Married her.

Christiana had stolen Lucius's heart. They had both shattered it.

A few months ago, the noxious rake had died in a scandalous accident, leaving *Lady Winfield* childless and alone. After the funeral, Lucius's flask had come out.

"Have you tried talking to her again?" Nettie asked, placing a hand on his arm as he tried to take another drink.

"She won't see me when I call or answer my letters. At the cemetery, she told me that men had been the cause of all her sorrows. She would never allow another into her heart." He put the flask away. "Got herself locked away on her mother's country estate."

His sister shook her head. "I'm sorry, but I'm sure she just needs time. Winfield was a terrible husband—"

"I tried to warn her. Of course, it only made me appear jealous of the knave." Lucius snorted, then handed Nettie the flask. "Take a nip. It will make the night pass faster."

She took a swallow and gasped, choking a bit. "Heavens, how can you drink this rot?"

"It's an acquired taste. It gets better with each swallow. Try again," he teased with a grin.

She shook her head and handed it back with a shiver. "I don't care for spirits. You know that."

"The more for me, then," he mumbled.

"Don't get foxed."

"Only mellow," he promised.

"Papa says it's time you start looking for your own wife. *She* may never come around, Lucius." Annette reached up on tiptoes and kissed his cheek. "Lady Jersey is introducing me to… someone, and I must dance the next quadrille with him. Please make sure you're back before eleven. Please, Lucius. Don't embarrass me by leaving me unchaperoned."

He sighed like a true martyr. "Of course. I'm your oldest brother. I will always protect you. Now go," he said, pushing her toward the stairs. "I'm crossing my fingers for you that he's handsome, plump in the pocket, and brave enough to face all your brothers."

This produced a snort from his sister, who promptly returned to the ballroom.

Lucius wasn't sure how long he sat there, drowning in his self-pity. But his flask was empty. Reason enough to return to the dance. It was a quarter of an hour before eleven. He poked his head inside, searching the room for Nettie. He saw her near the refreshments, her gaze scanning the occupants. *She's worried I won't make it.*

He cursed himself as he moved through the crowd, holding up a hand so Nettie would know he was there. Behind her, Lord Frederick—a well-known rapscallion in the clubs—approached his sister from behind. Another growl scraped his throat. The man better not touch her.

A knot formed in his stomach when Lord Frederick smiled. No, *leered*. Nettie's eyes went wide. The bloody nodcock had done something. Lucius saw him wink at a friend and extend his hand out again. Rage seared his chest as he yelled for his sister.

It happened so quickly. Nettie turned with a clenched fist and punched the cretin in the nose. Planted a perfect facer. His pride at her skill was cut short as chaos ensued. A deafening silence followed by a roar of gasps and murmurs. They gathered around her like vultures, the women whispering and pointing, the men smirking and nodding. Lord Frederick whined like the coward he was as red spurted from his nose, his finger wagging at Nettie as if she were the devil incarnate. Someone shouted for help.

Lucius couldn't help the slight smile. Justice, to be sure. But the consequences would be ruinous. He watched helplessly as Nettie offered Lord Frederick a handkerchief and was rebuffed like a leper. As Lucius pushed through the crowd, the remarks echoing throughout the room would soon be all over Town.

"Lord Frederick has been attacked!"

"Did Lady Annette plant him a facer?"

"Lecherous lickpenny? Such language!"

"She never did act a proper lady."

"Between her brothers and that right hook..."

"She's this Season's social pariah now."

Lucius reached his sister just as her courage faded. He gripped her elbow, silently cursing the panic in her eyes. "I-I..." The tears fell, and she hid her face in his coat.

Anger bubbled in his belly, sending heat to his face as he held Nettie close. "I saw what happened, you disgusting cur. To think a *lady* could take you out, you deuced molly," he yelled over her head.

"She's no lady," came the muffled response from behind a second bloody handkerchief. His blond hair was splattered with tiny droplets of cherry red, his weak chin thrust out indignantly.

"I *will* find you later and finish the job. Count on that." Lucius smiled thinly when Lord Frederick went even paler. Yes, he would find the rat and beat him soundly.

The crowd parted as they made their way to the door, indicating the need to distance themselves from the ruined lady and her brother. Lucius noticed her hands trembling, one tugging on his coat.

"I think I may—"

Lucius swept his sister into his arms as she fainted. His heart twisted again. This was his fault. If he'd been in the ballroom instead of drowning his sorrows, he would have stopped the duke's son. Nettie wouldn't be ruined.

***

One week later

White's Gentlemen's Club

"She's a hoyden." A nasal voice coming from the library. "If she were my daughter, I'd beat her soundly."

"Because you couldn't, eh?" asked another deeper voice. "She has a deuced good right punch, though I'd be more worried about her brothers."

"They're all bags of wind." Nasal man again. "I could take any of them in an honest fight. *If* they even knew how to play fair."

Lucius grinned. His friend, Mr. Hawkesbury, had done well. Pushing the library door open with a bang, he confronted Lord Frederick. It was difficult not to laugh at the man, his eyes still discolored and puffy from the facer Nettie had planted on him.

"Seems you've got a crook in your nose." Lucius strode toward the table by the window. "I'd be happy to straighten it out for you. Say, Jackson's tomorrow?"

"Wh-what are you babbling about?" Lord Frederick's tone was nonchalant, but his eyes held fear. "Didn't your mother teach you not to interrupt one's betters?"

Lucius snorted. "She did, along with the advice never to give in to a bully. Since my sister's lesson didn't seem to penetrate that thick skull, I shall have to reteach it."

"I would never lower myself—"

"To pinch a noble woman's arse? Your ship has sailed." Lucius turned to the others in the room. "Get The Book. First bet: Will Lord Frederick accept an invitation to a boxing match after saying publicly that I am merely a bag of wind? Or will the coward try to slink out with his tail between his legs, like the dog he is? Hurry, gentlemen, place those wagers while we wait with bated breath."

A blustering Lord Frederick rose, face and neck purple with rage, addressing his cohorts. The same men he'd agitated into arguments dozens of times, only to sit back and take the wagers himself. But today wouldn't end with a plump pocket and a smirk on the miserable lord's face. Lucius wanted justice, and by the devil, he'd have it.

"Does everyone hear this reprobate antagonizing me, goading me into a contest of fists? I'm not even healed yet, and he wants to take advantage—"

"Of a man who let a lady bust his nose," called out a patron from the back of the room.

"We all heard you boasting, Lord Frederick. Now prove your honor and accept the challenge," said Hawkesbury, sending a wink in Lucius's direction.

"You—you tricked me into saying it." The duke's son pointed at Hawk, who only shrugged his shoulders. He searched the crowd for a sympathetic face and only found the same murmuring that Nettie had received.

"Let's switch our wagers to how long the boy will whine."

"I say he'll run."

"My money is on him accepting—then not showing." Raucous laughter followed this comment.

"I do accept!" cried Lord Frederick.

In the end, no one would place a wager against Lucius to lose, so the last entry in White's betting book had been:

Lord Frederick, running from Lord Page's challenge—6; Lord Frederick accepting the challenge—4.

***

The match was brief. Lord Frederick had tried to insert a champion in his place, but when the man saw his opponent was Lucius, he returned the blunt. "Sorry, my lord, I didn't know it was you. I'd much rather watch this than participate."

As the two men faced one another, Lord Frederick made a fatal mistake in taunting his adversary. "Seems you have bad luck with women, Page. One stolen from you, one ruined while under your protection. You're gaining quite the reputation."

At the mention of Christiana, Lucius lost all control. He remembered his fist slamming into Lord Frederick's face, then being pulled from the floor, arms still swinging. The duke's son lay curled on his side, whimpering for mercy.

A week later, with Lord Frederick still in hiding while he

nursed his battered face, Lucius realized the satisfaction of pulverizing the man had been fleeting. In all honesty, it was his fault Nettie was ruined. He had allowed his self-pity to control his life, let the dark take over when he'd never been the gloomy type, hurting his beloved sister. It was time to put away the regrets. Either he made a plan or put Christiana from his mind. This brooding had cost Nettie her chance at a good match. If it took him the next ten years, he would keep his sister safe until she was married and under another's protection.

CHAPTER 1

November 1820
Falcon Hall, Suffolk

Christiana, Countess of Winfield, considered the package on her grandfather's large oak desk with a smile. Tomorrow was her birthday, and the package had arrived early—as it did every year. With slender fingers, she tugged at the string, then carefully opened the box. With a gasp, she withdrew the tiny china replica of a blue tit.

"It's beautiful, my lady," said her maid, Constance. "He never forgets, even after all these years."

"No," she murmured, rising from the desk and walking to the curio cabinet near the hearth. It held her most prized collectibles, though some of the contents were only precious to her. On the left were the porcelain vases her grandmother and mother had collected. One, a priceless Ming vase, was another sought-after possession. The Earl of Bentson had been pestering Christiana's mother to sell the piece for as long as she could remember. Once he discovered her daughter had inherited the vase, he turned his attention on the young widow.

She opened the right side of the cabinet and set the little bird among the others, all gifts from Lucius. She'd received the first, a swan, on her sixteenth birthday just before he left for university. Besides the short notes—carefully tied together and stored away in her chest—he had sent a new aviary specimen each November.

The goldfinch and capercaillie had arrived while he was away at university. Upon his return, she had been introduced to Lucius's friend, the Earl of Winfield. After a whirlwind romance, she'd agreed to marry him. Lucius had sent her a small wooden cuckoo that year.

A miserable year full of loneliness, tears, and regret. A husband who had lost interest once the prize had been won. A parade of lovers flaunted in her face. A score of mentions in the broadsheets. Humiliation, then the devastation of being a widow. A duel over another man's wife. She couldn't —wouldn't—face the *ton* after that.

Christiana had fled to Falcon Hall and never regretted escaping the cruelty of London and its inhabitants. She didn't care what others said about her once she was settled in the country. She was happy. Or reasonably so.

The following November, after coldly dismissing Lucius at Winfield's funeral, a package arrived. She had expected the clever Lord Page to send a crow, representing death or bad luck. Instead, Lucius had sent a golden eagle. His note had been simple yet layered with all the words unsaid.

Dearest Christiana,

I send you this golden eagle in the hope you will soar with your newfound freedom. It also embodies courage and rebirth. One is a quality you have always possessed. The other is my wish for you.

Your servant,

Lucius

Returning to the desk, determined to push the handsome viscount from her mind, she flipped through the correspondence. "Sir Horace Franklin is still asking to purchase her slate mines in Wales. And the Duke of Scuttleton has upped his offer on Vengeance."

"You crossed him when you outbid him on that horse. He won't give up until one of them is dead." The lady's maid pushed a dark curl back into her bun, peeking over her mistress's shoulder. "His Grace would offer a minor kingdom just to win him back."

Christiana chuckled. "Yes, he would. And then he'd beat the poor animal when it disappointed him." It had been an exhilarating day. Scuttleton had given his man a pouch and ordered him to use it all if necessary to buy the race horse. But she'd seen the scars on the duke's mounts, knew he was heavy on the whip and light on patience. Vengeance already wore the proof of previous abuse, and when the beast looked at her… Well, it had all been worth the harassment of the past year.

"Will you ever race him, my lady?"

"I don't know. He's fit again, and Jack feels he's ready to train. We'll see." Christiana drummed her fingers on the duke's note. "It's not about the money. It's about the unyielding power men feel they have. It's nice to thwart them when possible."

"It's become your life's pursuit." Constance shook her head as she picked up the letters ready to post. "You might try pursuing something else, something for pleasure instead of this vendetta."

"Horsefeathers! Vexing an arrogant man is great amusement. And I'm quite content with my life." She rested her chin on a fist and sighed. *Was she, though?* Yes, she supposed, most of the time. It was only the rare moments when alone in her room, or watching a couple dance a waltz with eyes only for each other, or gazing upon a brilliant sunset with no one to share its beauty. Those were the times she longed for a warm hand to join with hers, an arm around her shoulders to pull her close, soft lips...

Gracious, she was daydreaming. It had to be Lucius's gift. It always reopened the vacant corner of her heart. She'd dream of him tonight. His brown hair streaked with gold, those laughing green eyes, the chiseled jaw. The only kiss that had stirred her blood and made her feel safe and loved at the same time.

Enough! Thoughts of Lord Page only reminded her of the monumental mistakes she'd made. She needed to focus. Her neighbor was still pestering her about a piece of land between their properties he wanted to buy. It was part of the woods that acted as a boundary, and Lord Elwood had always used it for hunting before Christiana had arrived. In fact, she was certain he'd only asked her permission to hunt there as a courtesy, never expecting her to deny him the privilege.

He'd hounded her—pun intended—for the past five years. Elwood had tried flattery, flirtation, and then male dominance. Christiana was a conundrum to the earl. She didn't hunt, didn't invite guests to hunt, yet refused to let him or even consider allowing him to purchase it.

Watching Constance walk down the drive with the letters for post, she wondered about her future. She'd brought a basket to one of the tenants who'd just delivered a healthy baby. The infant had stirred something in her, made her wonder what it would be like to have a child of her own, a faithful man who loved her, a life beyond this antagonistic lifestyle she'd so carefully created.

Could she give up this game that had become her existence? The hatred she'd held inside for so long had dimmed.

Christiana had met men in the village who proved not all males were bombastic arses like her dead husband. She wandered to the curio cabinet and studied the collection of birds. No, not all men were the same.

Did she have the mettle to try again? Christiana shivered, remembering how she had pushed Lucius away at the funeral. Leaning into his strength would have been admitting he had been right about Edward, throwing away the little dignity she'd been able to retain after a horrendous marriage. Now…

Christiana shook her head to clear it of the memories. Enough melancholy, enough reminiscing. A new year would soon be upon them. If she could find a way to rid herself of these three niggling men after her properties, then she could think clearly about her future. But how could she eradicate them from her life without giving them what they want?

Returning to the desk, she took out a sheet of paper and dipped a fresh nib into the ink. The Widows League would have ideas. The members had come to her aid five years ago, assisting her with her widow's pension so she could be independent. Later, they helped her with the legal issues to retain her mother's estate. She still paid her quarterly dues, remaining a member to help other women who found themselves alone and without recourse except under another man's thumb.

Dear Lady Wyndam,

I hope this finds you well. I am enclosing my annual donation toward the Christmas fund, which has done so much for the women and children struggling through the winter. In addition, I thought you might help me with a predicament I find myself in...

When Christiana finished, she sprinkled the ink, flapped it a bit as her smile grew, then folded it. If there was a way to take care of these annoying gentlemen, the widows would come up with it. Such clever, helpful women. She always called on a few of them when in London.

With a loud sigh, she leaned back into the soft leather chair, her eyes straying to the porcelain, glass, and wooden birds in their case. Yes, it was time to move on. She would never be that innocent, naïve girl again, but she could find happiness, true happiness, couldn't she?

CHAPTER 2

22 December 1820
Beecham Manor, Suffolk

*L*ucius stuck his head out of the coach window. The tiger hopped down to open the black iron gate of the Beecham estate. He never tired of the view when returning home. A long gravel drive led up to a rambling mansion of limestone, its four stories and multiple gables shadowing the courtyard and portico. He knew every inch of the manor and the lands surrounding it. This was his inheritance, and he loved the place almost as much as he loved his family.

"Ready for some breakfast?" he asked his companions.

Fitzjames, a stocky blond fellow of medium height and a constant smile—or smirk, depending on the situation—gave a cheer. "Not used to getting up before the sun rises, Page. I'm usually heading home about then."

"True enough," agreed Hawkesbury, his friend who had

helped trap Lord Frederick. He was a tall man with reddish hair and blue eyes, fresh out of the army. "It's beginning to show on your face too. A little more sleep would do you good."

"I'll have time enough for that when I'm a doddering old man," Fitz said with a laugh. "Or when I take a wife." He added this with a glance at Lucius.

Both men had been invited to Beecham Manor for a few nights on their way to other destinations. But the real reason for the visit was his sister, Nettie. These were two gentlemen who were being considered as possible suitors for her. Fitz-james was the fourth son of a viscount. He had a good allowance and had made wise investments, allowing him to live the life of a gentleman without pursuing a career. Although he was a bit arrogant when it came to the ladies, Fitz was a good and honorable man.

Hawkesbury was the third son of an earl, had just sold his commission, and would inherit a small estate from his mother. He was also Lucius's pick out of the two, though he called them both friends. Neither would mistreat Nettie. But Fitz laughed at the idea of fidelity and would most likely have a mistress after marriage, where Hawk would never consider being unfaithful once he put on the leg shackles.

Gibbs greeted them at the top of the steps after sending footmen for their luggage. "Good day, Lord Page. It is good to have you home again," greeted the rotund butler in his typical monotone. "The family is in the breakfast room. Shall I have Cook send up more food?"

Not a mention of their early arrival, Lucius noted with a smile. The man was always perfectly manicured and never flustered. He hoped Gibbs lived forever, for there was no equal to their loyal butler.

"Yes, please. I'm afraid I roused these louts at dawn." He removed his gloves, greatcoat, and beaver hat, handing them to Gibbs. His ancestors frowned down upon them from the walls of the entryway. To the right were stairs leading to the first floor. "Come, my fine friends, and meet the Pages."

They entered the breakfast room, and his sister jumped from her seat. The man next to her, a friend of his father, grabbed the chair before it toppled backward.

"Lucius, I've missed you so!" squealed Nettie.

Lucius had barely made it through the doorway when he caught her and spun her around. "My sweet sister, I've missed you as well. And I've brought along some admirers." He planted a kiss on the top of her umber hair and set her back on her feet.

"May I introduce Mr. Hawkesbury," Lucius said, indicating the taller man, "and Mr. Fitzjames. You've both met my father, Lord Beecham. This is my father's fiancée, Lady Henney, and his good friend, Viscount Weston."

Nettie's eyes widened. "You know Lord Weston?"

"Of course, we've met at the club with Father when the Lords are in session," he answered, turning back to his friends. "And this is my lovely and inquisitive sister, Lady Annette."

She held out her hand. "It is a pleasure, sirs."

Lucius noted what appeared to be annoyance cross the viscount's face. With amusement, he wondered if he'd been mistaken. Could his father's friend be jealous of the newly arrived suitors? His father cut off Lucius's thoughts as he quit the table to give his son a slapping hug and shake hands with the new guests. "Welcome! Am I a day off or are you a day early? Doesn't matter, we've plenty of room."

"I wanted to send word but figured I'd get here on the tail of the messenger, so we thought to surprise you," Lucius explained, bending over Lady Henney's hand. "Ma'am, it's always a pleasure."

She blushed. "You get your charm from your father."

"That's why you love me so," he teased.

***

23 December 1820

Lucius thoroughly enjoyed watching his friends vie for his sister's attention. While Hawkesbury would appeal to Nettie's intellectual side, Fitzjames would be her match for outdoor activities. He had thought it would be entertaining to see who she favored more. But watching the group over the past two days, he'd noticed the glances between Nettie and Lord Weston. The viscount was a friend of Lucius's father, but they were not of the same age. Weston was younger, though there was still an age difference of close to twenty years between him and Nettie. Yet, there was true affection in their eyes when their gazes met.

He'd learned of the neighboring vicar's debacle of a visit. Lucius had thought the man was too weak-willed for Nettie, anyway. Hawk was out of the game after mentioning a possible move to India. Nettie would never be so far from her family. That left Weston and Fitz. Lucius would wager on the viscount.

After a rousing game of charades, with Hawk's clever guesses casting shadows over the slower but good-natured Fitz, the group decided to call it an evening. Lucius snuck down to the kitchen for another spoonful or two of custard. Since he was a boy, Cook had always put away an extra bowl or two for him in their "secret" place. At nine and twenty, he still snuck into the larder to find his stash of the golden sweet pudding.

After his snack, he headed for his room, humming "Good King Wenceslas." Tomorrow, his brother William would arrive with the final suitor. He hadn't met the man and wondered how he would compare to Weston and Fitzjames. As he passed the library, he heard a loud *thunk*. Peeking around the door, he saw Nettie standing over the prone form of Fitz, laughter bubbling from her.

He joined her. "Don't tell me he tried to kiss my sister, and she showed him her right hook." He crossed the room and stood beside her.

Annette shook her head as she caught her breath. "No, but he did kiss me." She wrinkled her nose. "I wasn't impressed. When he tried for a second, I sidestepped, and here we are."

Soon, they were both doubled over, wiping the tears from their eyes.

"What shall we do with him?" she asked as they both stared down at the snuffling mass.

"Leave him. He shouldn't drink so much when he's a guest. Let him wake up and wonder what the deuce happened." Lucius picked up a book from the floor, handed it to his sister, and put an arm around her shoulders as they left the library. "Blast, but the man has a snore that could wake the dead."

As they walked to their rooms, he kissed Annette on top of her head. He had seen his sister grow during their visit, shed the fear of men her own age, and come out of the shell she'd placed about herself. "I'm proud of you, Sister. I've seen my old Nettie come back to us in the past few days. Could one of my friends be the reason?"

Annette smiled up at him, and his chest swelled. It didn't matter who she chose if anyone. The light returning to those sea-green eyes was enough for him to know she would be well.

"I think the fact that they are your friends and know my history, yet still wanted to come, set me at ease. I've enjoyed myself the past two days, and I thank you. But one will live too far away, and the other really doesn't…"

"Make your heart go pitter-patter?" he asked, waggling his eyebrows.

She chuckled and shook her head. "Not a pitter or a patter."

"Hm. What of Lord Weston?" He halted and turned to her, wondering if she'd confirm his suspicion. "I've seen you watching him. And I know that look. Saw it in our brother Ambrose's eyes when he met Hester."

Embarrassment colored her cheeks. "I… I—"

"Does he cause a pitter or a patter?"

"Both," she gushed. "And he's also not as old as Papa."

Ah, she had worried about the difference in their years. But the expression on Nettie's face made his heart swell. Happiness. His sister was truly happy. Who cared how old the man was when he could put such a sparkle in her green eyes?

"It wouldn't matter. The heart doesn't have a calendar or follow age." He bent and whispered in her ear, "You know how long I have waited."

He thought of the woman he'd been unable to forget or replace. Yet, he had made the decision not to send her any more birthday trinkets. It was time to look ahead, find a compatible wife, and plan a future. He would be an earl someday; he had responsibilities. He had no more time to waste on romantic fantasies.

"Lucius, promise me something?"

"Depends." What was she up to with such an urgent tone?

"If I find a husband, will you open your heart to finding another to love?"

Lucius took in a deep breath. It was as if she'd read his mind. "I have committed myself to looking for a wife once you are settled. But love? I don't think another could steal my heart. Christiana is the only woman who sparks my soul."

CHAPTER 3

24 December

*L*ucius had overslept. Too many odd dreams. There had been a giant mistletoe, the berries taking on female faces, asking him to pick them for a kiss, choose one as a wife. But each time he plucked a berry, the face turned into Christiana's, and he dropped it, crushing it with his heel.

He inhaled the strong, bitter coffee, feeling his senses come back to life. As he was loading a plate with eggs and ham, his brother William and another gentleman entered.

"Brother," cried William, "it's good to see you again. My apologies for not being able to meet you at White's before you left London."

"Happy Christmas," Lucius said as they thumped one another on the back. "Have you just arrived?"

"Yes. We ran into Nettie and Weston outside." Will turned to the man beside him. "May I introduce Mr. Charles

Wilkens, whom I work with in London. If you ever need a solicitor, he's your man. Charles, this is my brother Lord Page."

"Mr. Wilkens." Lucius inclined his head. William was a barrister, and solicitors often required him to present a legal action for a client. But Will was supposed to be bringing the final suitor for his sister. "Where is…"

"The gentleman was unable to make it. However, I ran into Charles on his way to another house party. So, I convinced him to stay with us a night before he continued on to Falcon Hall." Will grinned, his hazel eyes twinkling as he mentioned the location.

Falcon Hall.

Lucius's head snapped up. "Are you well acquainted with Lady Winfield?" he asked, ignoring the mad thumping of his heart.

"No, my lord. My uncle, Sir Horace Franklin, has been trying to buy two slate mines from her. It's in Wales and close to two that he owns. She has put him off for over two years, and then he received an invitation to her estate over Christmastide." Charles shrugged. He was tall with brown hair, kind brown eyes, and a genuine smile. Lucius liked him immediately.

"It seems one must have a personal invite to be admitted. The wording is quite cryptic." Will grinned at his friend. "Would you mind showing it to him?"

Charles set down his satchel, opened it, and pulled out a thick lavender card with holly and ivy entwined around the edges. He handed it to Lucius.

Admits bearer to the private house party

Of the Countess of Winfield at Falcon Hall.

Guests shall arrive 24 December.

The competition for the desired prize begins 25 December thru 6 January.

Lady Winfield will only accept the proposal of the gentleman

Claiming victory of three or more challenges.

The favor of an answer is requested.

His mouth fell open. What was the chit up to? The vague wording of this left too many questions. Marriage? "Mr. Wilkens, I have questions *and* a proposition for you."

***

Falcon Hall, Norfolk

Christiana looked about the drawing room, happy with the decorations. Each room she would use for entertainment was festive with greenery, holly, and the scent of pine. But no mistletoe. It wasn't *that* kind of party. The Widows League had been instrumental in arranging this event. Lady Wyndam had written back within a week.

Dear Lady Winfield,

On behalf of the Widows League, I would like to thank you for your generous donation this year. We will be sure it helps those most in need.

As to your dilemma, several of us put our heads together. We believe the men should be given one final chance to obtain what they want from you. Some type of lottery or competition, but here's the twist: you are who they must beat. Only one of them will receive the prize—their desired property—the others will never bother you again with another request.

We assume from your correspondence that the only asset you are willing to part with is the Welsh property. You will have to be clever to make sure the appropriate contestant wins. However, this solves the issue of being further harassed by the others.

One thought to leave you with, my dear. Marriage would also solve this issue. A gentleman does not harangue another gentleman. It's bad form. Not that I am pushing any female in such a direction, just something to keep in mind. You are still young, beautiful, and full of life with many years ahead of you. Not all men are termagants.

I am confident your wit shall serve you well and provide us with a most entertaining recount the next we meet.

Your doting friend,

Katherine, Countess of Wyndam

Christiana folded the letter and slipped it inside her own copy of the invitation. The guests were due to arrive any time, and her challenges were in order. If all went well, Sir Horace Franklin would have his way. She didn't need the slate mines, and they were located next to those of the baronet. It was cumbersome dealing with the manager and the solicitor in Wales. The rest of her property and investments were handled by her solicitor in London. It was simpler to keep all her business under one roof, so to speak.

The money from the Welsh sale would provide a ready fund for the charities she continued to support and for the repairs and improvements needed in the village and around the estate. Some of the tenants would require new roofs this spring, and her steward wanted to expand planting to make the estate more self-sufficient.

After that, she intended to build a small aviary so she could listen to birdsong throughout the year. Christiana remembered the canary her father had bought her as a child. Watching the delicate creature behind the wires, singing for its freedom, had broken her heart. She could never again contain such grace and beauty in a tiny cage.

"The Duke of Scuttleton's representative has arrived, my lady," said the butler after knocking on the door. "I've shown him to his room, next to Lord Bentson, with instructions for dinner." He stood tall and lean in his dark suit, hands behind his back, silver temples blending into his raven hair. A scar formed an X near his right eye, and another down his left cheek was evidence of his years as a soldier, then pugilist, now butler and protector. "Sir Horace Franklin's man is also in residence. Lord Elwood sent word they will arrive this evening promptly at eight."

"Thank you, Mr. Jensen." She watched him turn to go. "Remember to stick to the plan."

"Of course," he said, rubbing one fist in his palm. "I shall always be within earshot. One untoward word, and I will make my presence known."

Christiana smiled. "I know you will."

Constance entered, reminding her it was time to dress for the evening. Once in her bedchamber, Christiana chose a simple silk gown of the palest rose, the square bodice cut low and beaded with tiny pearls, the same pattern repeated on the puffed sleeves and hem. A sheer gossamer shawl of cream, a pearl pendant, and earbobs completed her outfit.

"You're lovely, my lady," her maid gushed, poking another pearl hairpin into Christiana's loose chignon. "The men will be sorry you are not the prize."

"I suppose the rumors are running rampant in London by now. *That wicked Lady Winfield making men compete for her hand. And at her home, unchaperoned.* I do enjoy a good on-dit when I'm the one who started it." She blew out a breath and glanced at the clock on the mantel. "I suppose it's time."

"The sacrificial lamb to the slaughter." Constance giggled as she stepped away from her mistress. "I will say the gentleman who came in the baronet's place is very handsome. It won't be a hardship playing up to him."

Christiana took a deep breath and smoothed her skirt. *You can do this.* She opened the door to the drawing room, and Constance followed her, taking a seat in a corner of the room. Three men and an older lady stood in front of the hearth, drinks in hand. The elderly gentleman, with a rounded belly, wiry gray sideburns, and a thick head of gray hair, smiled as she entered. "Lord Bentson, how good of you to come in person. I hope your journey was uneventful."

"Yes, ma'am," he said, his voice gravelly from age. "If the outcome is favorable, putting up with the cold will be worth it."

"Lord and Lady Elwood, are you coping well with these frosty temperatures?" she asked her neighbors.

"Aye, my lady" replied the viscount, tugging the too-small waistcoat back down after bowing over Christiana's hand. "It's a short distance to come for something so valuable."

The viscountess, a plump woman with a round face and soft brown eyes, frowned. "I must admit it's a good thing I'm here. You might have been alone with all these gentlemen."

"Which is why I'm so grateful for your attendance." Christiana had always wondered if her neighbors had been a love match or an arranged marriage. Lady Elwood was kind and always looked on the bright side of a matter. Her husband seemed to wear a perpetual frown, his dark brows usually drawn in a V. Two mismatched souls or did opposites attract?

"Since we can't see the grandchildren this year, I was so happy to receive the invitation. I believe we shall have a monstrous good time." She beamed at them all, her extra chin wobbling a bit as she nodded her head.

"And…" Christiana faltered, not knowing the third man. "I'm afraid we have not yet been introduced."

"May I introduce Lady Winfield?" Bentson intervened. "This is one of the Duke of Scuttleton's lads, Lord Frederick."

Lord Frederick, a short man with thinning blond hair and barely a chin, stepped forward. His clothes were well tailored but loud. The stripes on his blue and white waistcoat were too wide, his cravat too big, his lace cuffs too long. Too many gems winked in his extra-large neck pin, a ring on each finger. He bent over her hand and brushed her gloved knuckles with his lips. "I'm hardly a lad, Bentson, at eight and twenty."

"Very true," agreed the old man, "and you've less hair than I do." He winked at Christiana.

She'd forgotten how much she liked the earl. In truth, she had always wondered if he and her mother had only used the excuse of the Ming vase to continue their correspondence. But her mother was gone now, and Christiana would never know.

Lord Frederick let out a loud yawn and stretched his arms above his head, a sneer—or was it supposed to be a smile?—on his face as he asked, "I do hope you have some titillating amusements planned for us over the next few days. It was quite a sacrifice to leave Town this time of year."

Christiana raised a brow. "I will do my best, sir, though *titillating* might not be the appropriate word." She glanced about the room. "We are missing someone. Has anyone seen the fourth guest?"

"I'm right here, my lady," said a deep tenor from the direction of the door behind her.

Her heart stopped. It had been years since she'd heard the voice, and it sent heat racing from her neck to the tip of her toes. *It couldn't be.*

"The bloody devil," whispered Lord Frederick, growing pale.

"No, I'm just Lord Page, though a cur like you must see the devil over his shoulder on most days." Lucius pushed away from the doorjamb and approached the fireplace. "Looks like fine French brandy. I think I'll have a glass. Lady Winfield, may I pour you one?"

Christiana managed a nod, realizing too late she shouldn't indulge in such strong spirits. The man had grown more handsome. How was that possible? The candlelight danced gold upon his thick brown hair, slightly longer than fashionable and curling at the nape. The superfine coat stretched across his broad shoulders as he handed her the crystal glass. His trousers a perfect fit around his muscular thighs. She dragged her eyes back up to his face, seeing the laugh lines crinkle around the emerald-green orbs dancing with mischief.

Her mouth went dry, her tongue as thick as a sheep's wool in winter. She could only nod, wondering if her fingers would be able to hold the drink and thinking a *bottle* of brandy might be best.

CHAPTER 4

ONCE UPON A WIDOW©

*L*ucius smiled, hoping his racing pulse couldn't be seen. It had been so long since he'd seen her, been in the same room, breathed the same air. How had she grown more beautiful? And how would he keep himself from pulling her into his arms and ravaging those soft, full lips?

Ironically, it was Bumbling Broken Nose who saved the hour and redirected the attention away from Lucius.

"How the devil did this ingrate get an invitation?" demanded Lord Frederick. "I refuse to spend one night under the same roof as this... this... *man.*" His mottled face trembled with rage, and Lucius was certain the nodcock didn't realize he was rubbing his nose.

"It seems the bump on it is gone," observed Lucius with a smirk. "Did I knock it straight on the second go-round?"

Lady Winfield's delicate golden brows drew together.

She doesn't know.

"Lord Frederick, if you would like to forfeit and leave, that is your prerogative. I'm not sure what instructions your father gave you," said the countess, looking back and forth between Lucius and the duke's son.

"Yes, I'm sure he'll understand if you tuck tail and run," added Lucius. "Again."

"Why you..." Lord Frederick took a step forward, his fists clenched, then hesitated.

"Yes?" He arched one brow, also moving forward a step and crossing his arms.

"Lord Page, please be civil," admonished Lady Winfield. "He is a guest in my home."

"Yes, that's your misfortune." Lucius turned to Broken Nose with a forced smile. "Shall we call a truce for the time we are here?"

"I-I..." He looked around for support, found none, then huffed, "I suppose. But keep your fists to yourself."

"Lord Page will be the epitome of courtesy," assured the countess. "But I suggest you don't provoke him."

When she turned her head away, Lucius saw she was holding back a smile. "Now that we're all present, shall I give you an outline of the activities to come?"

Everyone murmured their agreement. He moved next to Christiana, breathed in her sweet vanilla scent, and waited for her to take a seat. So he could plant himself beside her. His confidence returned as he took measure of his competition. Whatever this game was, unless the winner was determined by being the oldest or the most ridiculous, he felt he could win any type of competition against the men present.

Christiana sat on the edge of a chaise longue, and Lucius stepped around her, cut off Broken Nose, and settled himself next to the lady. "There's a bit more room if you'd like to join us," Lucius said to Lord Frederick, patting the velvet cushion on his other side. "We could reminisce about old times."

Lady Winfield pressed her lips together to hold back the laughter, but Lady Elwood let out an unladylike guffaw. "I remember! Your nose…" She pointed at Lord Frederick. "His sister…" She pointed at Lucius. "Lud, I wish I had been there. What a sight to see a whip of a girl—"

"Ma'am, as much as I would like to relive *parts* of the event, perhaps we should let the lady proceed? You and I can continue this conversation later over the wassail bowl." He grinned. "I'll tell you what didn't come out in the broadsheets."

Lady Winfield cleared her throat, smoothed her perfectly coiffed hair with only a slight tremble in her hand, and swallowed. "Yes," she agreed.

"You are even lovelier when your cheeks color," he murmured, noticing she refused to look in his direction though they sat close enough to feel the heat coming off her in waves.

"Yes," she said again. "I mean…" She scooted over, hugging the end of the chaise longue. "I have arranged a series of contests. Each of you will have one marker to use if you wish to pass on a challenge. After that, if you forfeit, you are out of the competition. The first gentleman who wins at least three challenges will be the victor."

"And if no one takes three challenges?" asked Elwood.

"Then no one wins," she answered with a sweet smile. "I shall keep all my possessions, and I will never be bothered again to sell them to you."

"Let me see if I understand this." Lucius's gaze traveled over her face, wondering how the chit hadn't aged a day. "We are all to compete against one another—and you—and only the victor gets his desired prize?"

He held her ice-blue gaze, watching it soften, melt as she nodded. He wanted to lift his hand and stroke his knuckles down her cheek. A slow smile curved his lips. *Brilliant.*

"How many events are there?" asked Lord Elwood. "If this involves namby-pamby activities like embroidery, then—"

"Then you'll do your best and try not to poke your finger with the needle," interrupted his wife. "Lady Winfield, this is the most ridiculous, the most outlandish idea I've heard in years. Thank you so much for inviting us. I only wish we didn't have to take the carriage back and forth each day."

"There is plenty of room, ma'am, if you'd like to stay when you return tomorrow. I'd be happy to prepare another bedchamber." Lady Winfield gave Lucius a side-glance. "And to answer your question, Lord Elwood, there are nine games if we finish them all."

"Well, I'm here for the duration," announced Lucius, leaning back and stretching his arm across the back of the couch. He noticed Christiana's intake of breath and the sudden rigidity of her back. He was making her uncomfortable. *Good.* "Nothing could drag me away."

"Me either," spouted Broken Nose. "I shall best everyone here."

Lord Elwood harrumphed, his jowls jiggling about his neck, his mouth turned down.

"I may be an old man, but there are still some things I can manage if the goal is valuable enough." Lord Bentson slapped his knee. "Hounds teeth, but this will be a jolly good Christmastide."

***

After dinner, Christiana and Lady Elwood retired to the drawing room. As soon as the tea was poured, Lady Elwood began the interrogation.

"You do realize your invitation, if seen by the wrong eyes, could be interpreted as you being the prize. Marriage to the victor." The viscountess's eyes glittered. "Any side bets being placed?"

Christiana's face heated, thinking of how close Lucius had been on the chaise longue. She could almost feel the heat coming off his body, scrambling her thoughts. After five years of only annual notes accompanied by his token of "remembrance," why did his presence affect her so?

"I want you to know I do not give a fig if my husband wins or not. This is such a clever game. Do all these men want that strip of property for hunting?"

Christiana laughed. "No, each contestant wants something different from me. I've grown weary of the constant attention and thought this would be an entertaining way to end it."

"What else is on the table?"

"An antique, a horse, and two slate mines."

"Ooh, let me see if I can match the prize with the man." Lady Elwood tapped her lips with her pointer finger. "The young man, Lord Frederick, wants the horse. He seems the type who would ride a poor beast until it dropped." Her brown eyes widened. "I didn't mean to insult the man. But a weak man will always take his frustrations out on those below him, especially women and animals."

Christiana nodded. "He is here for the horse, though it's his father who has been pestering me for it. And the reason you mentioned is exactly why I outbid the duke."

"You bought the beast at auction? Such courage, going on your own like that." She patted Christiana's hand. "I like you more and more, my dear. Now, what do Lords Page and Bentson want? Hmm."

In truth, Christiana wasn't sure either. Although Lucius said he was here for Sir Horace, she couldn't understand how it had come about. How did he know the baronet? Why would the man trust Lucius to negotiate for the slate mines?

"I could see Bentson wanting either prize," decided Lady Elwood. "But if I had to choose, I would say he was more the collector at his age."

"You are very clever. And Lord Page is here for the mines."

Lady Elwood looked over Christiana's shoulder. "If that's what you want to tell yourself, my dear."

"Ladies," called Lucius from the doorway, the butler behind him. "The gentlemen are waiting in the billiards room."

Lady Elwood followed Mr. Jensen down the hall, leaving her alone with Lord Page.

Horse feathers! Lucius had taught her billiards. He would surely win this contest, and she'd been so sure the party would start with a victory for her.

To her surprise, he retrieved the red card from his pocket. "Would you like me to pass on this one?"

"Only if you want to," Christiana said airily, as if it really didn't matter. As she went to pass him, his hand on her arm stopped her.

Lucius reached inside his coat and pulled out a sprig with a berry on it, holding it above her head. "I brought this from home."

She peered above her, then at him, then at her velvet slippers. "Lord Page..." But in that heartbeat of hesitation, he slanted his head and brushed his lips across hers. A lightning strike straight to the heart. Her body tingled, right down to the good bits. She blinked, looking up at him, her mouth open.

He leaned down to whisper in her ear, "I would like to challenge you to a private competition. Each one will begin at the stroke of midnight. Tonight, meet me in the kitchen."

His deep-green eyes searched hers, his gaze sweeping over her face as if memorizing it. Then one hand cupped her cheek, and he kissed her again. This time, he pulled her close with his free hand, and Christiana knew she would have melted into a puddle if he hadn't held her so tightly. It was over as quickly as it had begun—without warning. She was vaguely aware of his chuckle, but when she opened her eyes, he was gone.

Standing there for a few minutes, her fingers on her lips, she tried to remember the last time she had felt any kind of passion. It had been so long. But now her body was a roiling tempest, and she could only pray to weather this storm building inside her.

CHAPTER 5

ONCE UPON A WIDOW©

Midnight in the kitchen

ucius sat in a wooden chair before the large, scarred table in the kitchen. He had a way with cooks, and his charm had worked again tonight. The delightful lady, Mrs. Harding, was happy to be his accomplice.

The fire from the large cooking hearth spread a golden glow about the room. Rosemary, garlic, and lavender hung from the beams in a corner of the kitchen, their faint scents mixing together sweetly. A candle, next to a bottle of madeira and two glasses, flickered on the table, casting dancing shadows across the walls. On a side table were fresh biscuits and orange slices.

"Do not think I came only because you ordered me to." She stood in the doorway, her hair pulled back, a simple black gown on with a thick wool shawl. "But I have questions."

"Yes, I thought you might." He stood and held out a hand. "I promise, no more hidden mistletoe. Unless you bring it."

She smiled and shook her head. "Will you get me foxed and have your way with me?"

He barked out a laugh. "Tempting as it sounds, no. Please, sit." He held out a chair and pushed it in slightly as she settled into it. He resumed his seat beside her. "I thought we'd play a game of Truth or Lie."

"What does that involve?" One hand fisted her shawl close to her chest, the other lay clenched in her lap. "And how did you come by my invitation?"

"Ah, it seems the good baronet sent his unmarried nephew to claim his mines. His wife didn't want him gone over Christmastide. Especially to the home of a young widow with a somewhat questionable reputation." He tipped his head, studying her. "I convinced him that, as we were old friends, I might have the upper hand in negotiations."

"I've explained the purpose of this house party." Her eyes took on a cerulean shade in the soft glow. "And what have you heard about my reputation?"

"Rampant speculation about the first three Christmas parties. Masquerades, mistletoe in every dark corner, promises made, promises broken."

"Hmm." She tilted her head, imitating him. "Sounds like a typical ball in London."

"The last one was particularly interesting. It was said only males were invited, and you chose one to be your lover for the year." Lucius unclenched his jaw. He had punched the baron who'd told him the rumor. Apologized, of course, and gave the poor man his box at the theater for the Season. "Then last year, nothing. Not a peep from Falcon Hall. Was your prize so magnificent that you kept him an extra year?"

Christiana laughed. A boisterous laugh. Not a hint of

spite in it, just genuine mirth. "Well, the broadsheets haven't changed in five years, I see."

"Did you think they would?" He chuckled too, the knot in his stomach loosening. He'd known, deep down, the on-dits couldn't be true. "What did happen at those parties if you don't mind telling me?"

She studied him for a moment, her gaze lingering on his mouth, down his neck, his chest, lower... then back to his face as her clear blue eyes locked with his. A fierce heat fired straight to his core. The devil, if she wasn't as stunning as that night he'd first kissed her. More so. As if time had decided to improve on the original.

"I admit the first two were a bit raucous. I invited arrogant men and independent, brazen women. I will only say the females won the day, sending the pompous males home with their prides bruised." Her lips quirked up. "It was magnificent."

This explained a great deal. The coves who attended had either seemed hesitant to talk about it or bragged so blatantly about their conquests that Lucius knew they were lying. One even said he'd been sworn to secrecy. Lucius realized they'd all been embarrassed. But since the first lot hadn't revealed their "defeats," she'd been able to lure a second group the next year. "So did you run out of vindictive ladies the third year?"

Christiana shook her head, the honied waves curling across her shoulders. "A friend of mine, who had been ill-treated by several *gentlemen*, wanted retribution. I invited those men, and she proceeded to blackmail each one. They received their due—or lost it, I should say—and she is now living happily in Italy."

His eyes widened. She had nerve, always had. Her strength had appealed to him once. Now it excited him. He would proceed with caution. "One of them must have started the rumor about you choosing a lover, then."

"Or they all conspired to lie. It doesn't matter. I don't care what is said about me in Town."

"Nor do I." He leaned forward, curling his fingers into his palm to keep from reaching out and touching a silken amber lock. "Shall we start the game?"

Christiana nodded, eyes narrowed, interested. "The rules, my lord?"

"I say something about you. If it's true, you take a drink of wine. If it's not, I take a drink. Very simple." He poured two fingers of madeira into each glass and pushed one toward her.

"Nothing about Lord Page is simple." But her lips held a slight smile. "You start."

"Gladly." He rubbed his chin as if considering what to say, though he'd run this scenario through his head a dozen times. "You were never truly in love with Edward."

She snorted and picked up the glass, taking a sip. "You believed those rumors about me."

"You'll have to be more specific," he said with a grin.

"You believed I took a lover."

He groaned and threw back the contents of the glass. "I will say in my defense that, having experienced the passion of your kiss, I couldn't imagine you remaining celibate."

Christiana's stare made him want to fiddle with his cravat. What was she thinking?

"Lucius, we had only chaste kisses between us until…" She looked away, chewing on her bottom lip. "If you had always kissed me like you did the last time, when you tried to change my mind about Edward, I might not have married."

A punch to the gut. "I was playing the gentlemen."

"And he played the rogue. Rogues are always more

41

romantic and thrilling than gentlemen. Especially to an innocent who doesn't understand how men lie." She shook her head. "Our last kiss was…"

"What?" He remembered how he'd danced her out of the ballroom that night after Edward had announced their engagement. Begged her not to trust him, then kissed her with all the repressed passion and years of longing spilling from his heart.

"I never felt such… passion with Edward. His words titillated my senses, not his kisses or… You found your voice too late. I'd already accepted." Christiana sighed. "And now here you are, making me remember what took me years to forget."

Lucius leaned back, satisfied with the answer. "You're lonely."

She nodded. He tapped her glass. With a chuckle, she took another sip. Spotting the nearby snack, she said, "I see you've already charmed Mrs. Harding."

"Lovely woman. She's very fond of you."

"You think you still love me."

His breath caught at the suddenness of the statement. But she was wrong. He tapped her glass again. Was that disappointment in her eyes? He grinned. "I *know* I still love you. I've never stopped."

She blinked at him but said nothing.

"You don't believe I can convince you." He would call her bluff.

She tapped his glass. "I have every confidence you can."

He poured himself more wine and drank it in one gulp. "You're afraid to risk your heart."

"It's my turn, I believe."

Clever chit, avoiding the statement.

"You still hate Edward and believe I betrayed you."

This wasn't going the way he'd planned. He grabbed the bottle and took a long drink, not bothering with the glass.

"I'm not sure if it's still so strong as hate. Time and death have a way of blurring the edges, but I will never forgive him for taking what was mine."

"I *belong* to no one." Christiana stood and retrieved the plate of biscuits and oranges. "You still have a penchant for these?" she asked as she popped a slice of the fruit into her mouth.

Lucius watched as her lips closed around the segment. "You are afraid to risk your heart again."

With a sigh, she picked up her glass and took a drink, licking her lips. "Madeira pairs well with orange." She closed her eyes, her head tipping back. "You cannot understand why I still shy away from men."

He went to pick up his glass, but her hand dashed out to stop him. "No, not part of the game. An observation."

They were talking again as they once had. No reservations, no correct words to be chosen, only the simple truth as they knew it. "Some men should always be shied away from. But you had a kind father, a model from which you learned not all men are thoughtless or cruel."

"But he died. Followed too early by my mother, who couldn't find happiness on her own." Her sorrowful eyes held his. "I'm not sure which is worse—being ignored and humiliated by your husband, or being so in love, you do not wish to live without him. Either way, a woman has little choice."

"So you prefer to be alone?" A waste, in his opinion. "You have so much to give, Christiana. Let me help you do that.' She looked away, and he pressed his point. "If you give me a chance, you will see I can make your life better. Fall in love with me, don't fall in love with me. It matters not. After the past five years, you already know you can live without me. Where is the risk, then?"

"What do you propose?"

Hope sprung in his chest. "We'll have our own competition in the dark of night while the others sleep. If I win the most challenges, you will allow me to court you. With an open heart, not merely tolerating my presence. If you win, I shall never shadow your doorstep again."

She drummed her fingers on the table. "That's why you kissed me earlier. To remind me of the passion missing in my life." Her gaze returned, searching his face for something, an expression between longing and doubt in her green depths.

He smiled and reached out to cover her hand with his own. "Will you allow me the chance to show you the man I've become? To reacquaint myself with the woman I fell in love with?"

A heavy sigh, a bittersweet smile. "I fear I'm more disillusioned with love than hesitant. So, midnight tomorrow? Here?" Christiana stood, preparing to leave.

He did the same, wanting another kiss before she left him. Another memory to add to the earlier kiss as he tried to find sleep later.

"No, tomorrow night we'll meet in the drawing room." He moved closer and cupped her cheek in his palm. She pressed into it, and it was an almost impossible feat not to pull her close, feel her body meld with his. As he leaned forward to taste her lips, her hand reached out, and the glass of madeira went crashing to the floor. She let out a cry as it shattered on the stone floor.

The butler burst into the kitchen, chest heaving as he scanned the room and found his employer and then Lucius. With bunched fists, the giant of a man marched toward him, eyes narrowed, violence in his demeanor.

"I'm fine, Mr. Jensen. Just an accident," said Christiana, one arm out to stop the butler. She turned to Lucius. "I will see you in the morning, Lord Page. I hope you sleep well." And with that, she left the kitchen, her defender close on her heels.

No wonder she had no fear of hosting unattached men. Christiana was no fool. The brute would make short work of most men who threatened his mistress. And judging by Jensen's face, he had no issue with receiving pain while inflicting it. His loyalty was obvious. And Lucius's heart felt lighter at the realization.

CHAPTER 6

25 December

*C*hristiana stretched and yawned. For the first time in years, she had slept through the night. As a child, her mother had always commented how she slept so soundly, nothing but the house on fire could wake her. But after her wedding, sleep had evaded her. Most nights, she woke and sat by the fire. Reading a nice dull text sometimes helped to make her lids heavy once again. Other times, Constance would hear her and bring some warm milk.

This morning, she threw back the counterpane, her toes scrunched on the plush wool rug as she slid off the mattress. The sun was just peeking through the slit in the drapes, and she pulled them back, enjoying the pinks and purples melting together on the horizon.

"You're bright as a ray of sunshine this morning," said Constance, coming from the small connecting room where she slept. "Did you sleep well? I was afraid after meeting with Lord Page, you might be even more restless."

She shook her head. "I feel like I could conquer the world. I cannot remember the last time I was this refreshed." Christiana whirled to face her maid, her long waves trailing around her. "A new day. What surprises await us, do you think?"

Her maid laughed. "I like this new mistress of mine. Is this what you were like when you were a girl?"

Christiana considered, her lips in a pout. "If I remember correctly, yes." Then she beamed at Constance. "I believe this may be my last party. I shall achieve my goal and leave the past where it belongs—in the past."

"Very fine advice, my lady. Now, drink your chocolate before it gets cold while l brush your hair."

As she sipped her sweet drink, her body humming to life, she went over her time spent with Lucius in the kitchen. She had missed him. His face was like a shining beacon of happiness, reminding her there was still joy in the world. When she woke this morning, the heaviness blanketing her, a constant companion, was lighter, easing its weight upon her shoulders. Did she have Lucius to thank for that? The next few days would tell.

***

Late afternoon after attending church, Lord and Lady Elwood arrived with two trunks. "We've accepted your generous offer to stay, my dear," called the viscountess from the steps of the carriage. She pulled her fur-lined cloak together with one hand and extended the other to her husband, who waited on the ground to assist her. The feather on her hat bobbed up and down as she descended. "I've been at sixes and sevens wondering what the challenge would be today."

The butler ordered the footmen to retrieve the luggage,

and he showed the couple to their shared room. When they returned to the drawing room, Christiana was serving tea. "Lady Winfield," asked Lord Elwood, "my wife and I were discussing this… unusual venture last night. We wondered if I was the only one to participate, or if my wife could take my place on occasion?" His dark-brown eyes held hope while he rubbed the back of his neck. "Act as one, in a sense."

She studied his round, ruddy face, then nodded. "I will allow it."

The viscountess clapped her hands. "Lud, this will be entertaining. What is on for today?"

"First, we light the Yule log." She took the tinder box from the mantel. Kindling had been arranged under and on top of the huge log. The smoky scent soon blended with the aroma of pine and rosemary.

As the flames licked at the thin sticks and branches, she turned back to her guests. "Since it is Christmas, we will play parlor games. A game of whist between four, then one game for the winning partners to decide who will gain a point for the day."

"Shall we put a bit of coin on the game to make it more interesting?" asked Lord Frederick in a bored tone.

"Because this entire scheme isn't remarkable enough?" asked Lord Page.

Christiana had almost forgotten his dry wit. Lucius had dressed in a festive red-and-black pinstripe waistcoat with black trousers and a black coat. His brown hair was combed back, the light from the windows highlighting the golden streaks. Her heart skipped a beat when he stared at her unapologetically, a corner of his mouth kicked up a tiny bit in an almost-smirk.

Lord Frederick rolled his eyes, and Lord Bentson rubbed his hands together, his faded hazel eyes coming to life. "It's been awhile, but I was quite the man at the table when I was younger. Would you care to partner with me, Lady Winfield?"

She hid her grin when the older man's suggestion caused Lucius and Lord Frederick to gawk at one another in horror. "I will sit this one out, my lord, so we have an even number."

The elderly man turned to the Elwoods. "Who is the chosen player between the two of you?"

"I am," said Lady Elwood. "He's never had much luck with cards."

"Then will you do me the honor of being my partner?" he asked, wiggling his thick gray brows.

"I'd be delighted."

"Bollocks," muttered Lord Frederick, rubbing his paunch as if he'd had a bit of spoiled beef.

"As much as I'd like to win, I want him to lose more," Lucius whispered in her ear as he passed her on his way to the table. "Unless you tell me otherwise."

She pressed her lips together, not allowing the sigh to escape from the warmth of his breath against her neck. "Best out of three?" she asked the group instead.

The guests murmured and nodded in agreement. Cups of wassail were passed around while Christiana and Lord Elwood pulled up chairs to sit near the players. At one point, as Lucius decided which card to start the round with, Lord Frederick kicked his partner under the table, followed by a wide-eyed look across the pile of cards.

"Was that a spasm, you imbecile, or did you mean to kick me?" asked Lucius, the incredulous expression on his face almost comical. "And what's wrong with your eyes? Are you in pain? Constipated?"

This sent Lady Elwood into a fit of giggles, Lord Bentson chuckled and slapped his knee, and Lord Frederick's face was so red, Christiana was sure steam would erupt from the top of his head.

"I think he was trying to tell you he has trump," Lord Elwood said in a loud whisper, a hand covering one side of his face, then snickered.

The first game went to Lady Elwood and Lord Bentson, an embarrassing whitewash with Lord Frederick and Lord Page receiving no points. Christiana almost felt sorry for Lord Frederick, knowing he would never win with Lucius as his partner, and knowing he could never prove the loss was deliberate.

Lucius and Lord Frederick barely won the second. "Hounds teeth, Page, how do you manage to win at White's and play so miserably here?" asked Lord Frederick, his jaw clenched. "Pay attention, will you?"

"Why, my lord, how rude. Did your mother teach you any manners?" Lord Page gasped, assuming an innocent expression. "I can only imagine it is my partner's lack of skill."

Lord Frederick's icy blue eyes narrowed. "Don't antagonize me. You'll be sorry."

Lucius chortled, apparently not the least concerned. "Are you threatening me?" His hand went to his chest, his eyes toward the ceiling. "Without my sister here to defend me? Heaven help us."

"Gentlemen, we have a game to focus on," intervened Lord Bentson. "You can argue outside rather than in front of the ladies—after we've soundly beaten you."

The third was taken with ease by the first couple. "If I didn't know how competitive you were, I'd say you lost on purpose," grumbled Lord Frederick, casting a sour glance at Lucius who only continued to grin.

"We all have bad days," he answered with a shrug.

Bentson slapped his knee. "Dash it, but I haven't enjoyed myself so much in years. My thanks, Lady Winfield, whether I get the vase or not."

"What vase?" asked Lord Frederick. "I'm here for a horse."

"And I'm here for a piece of hunting property that butts up to mine," said Lord Elwood.

"It's no wonder the poor dear is hosting this competition with so many dunderheads pestering her." Lady Elwood winked at Christiana. "What is your heart's desire, Lord Page?"

He grinned, picking up on the viscountess's innuendo. "I'll keep my personal desires to myself. But as far as this contest, I'm representing a merchant from London for two slate mines in Wales."

"What will Lady Elwood and I have to do in order to declare a winner tonight?" asked Lord Bentson, sinking slowly into a leather chair before the hearth. "Please, no needlepoint. My eyes are terrible for any close work, though my spectacles are in my room."

"Heavens no." Christiana gave a pointed look at a shallow silver bowl near the wassail. "A bit of snapdragon. Whoever pulls the most raisins from the flaming brandy."

"Oh-ho!" cried the elderly man with glee. "Not much feeling left in these old digits. I'm afraid I'll have a leg up on you, Lady Elwood."

"It's neither here nor there," she answered good-naturedly. "It's all about the playing, not about the winning."

"So says the woman with nothing to lose," mumbled her husband.

Carolers from the village arrived and sang several of Christiana's favorites, including "God Rest Ye Merry Gentlemen." They shared the remaining wassail after several lovely songs. After dinner, Lord Bentson was true to his word and won snapdragon. Lady Elwood pulled three raisins from the fiery bowl and announced she was too delicate to continue. This sent her husband into guffaws, and Lord Elwood proceeded to snatch two more of the raisins, giggling with each pull and smacking his lips as he chewed the tiny plump fruit.

"One point to Lord Page for billiards and one point to Lord Bentson for whist and snapdragon," declared Lady Elwood. Her cheeks were pink from the wine at dinner and the wassail.

"Please thank your cook for a delicious meal," said Lord Bentson. "The goose was roasted to perfection. And the plum pudding…" He rubbed his belly. "Well, I ate too much of it if that tells you anything."

"She'll be pleased to hear it." Christiana gave Lucius a side-look. She had been so curious as to why he had come that she hadn't asked about his family yet. Tonight, while they… What challenge did he have planned for her?

CHAPTER 7

ONCE UPON A WIDOW©

Midnight in the drawing room

*L*ucius paced before the hearth, embers still glowing and popping as he looked at the clock again. *She's late. She's not coming.* He ran a hand through his hair, then walked to the side table, and poured himself a brandy. She looked beautiful today. And more relaxed. He'd made her laugh several times, and the wariness in her corn-flower-blue eyes had faded for a moment.

What would he do if she didn't come? Pound on her bedchamber door? Visions of Christiana in a robe with little else beneath put him in a tailspin. He threw back the brandy and poured another.

"Courage for the upcoming battle?"

Her sultry tone cast a net over him. He stood with his back to her, his eyes closed, imagining her coming up behind him and sliding her arms around his middle. *Dunderhead.*

"Well, I'm here. What devious scheme have you decided upon for this eve—morning?"

Lucius turned. Christiana stood before the fire, the golden light shimmering against the deep-blue velvet of her dress. Her bodice was trimmed with tiny paste diamonds, drawing attention to her full bosom. The skirt clung to her curves as she moved toward him, a smile turning up her plump pink lips. He wanted to pull the diamond hairpins from her hair, letting the thick tresses fall across her shoulders like a wave of liquid amber.

He drew in a steadying breath. "Since your challenge was cards, I thought I'd follow your lead for the rest of the time. Do you care for cribbage?"

"I do. We can talk while we play." She walked to a shelf along the back wall and fetched a board and pegs. "I hope your family is doing well?"

Lucius shook his head. "Annoying but wonderful as always. Wine?" He poured her a glass when she nodded.

They settled at the table and took turns cutting the deck. He pulled the ten of spades, but she won the deal with the two of hearts. She shuffled the cards, then offered him the chance to cut the deck. He declined with a grin. "You wouldn't cheat at a game of the heart."

She laughed, a delicious sound that tickled his insides. "My sister said to give you her love."

"How is Lady Annette? I miss her and her humor." Christiana dealt them each five cards, then they each discarded two face down, forming the crib. She reached across the table and laid her hand on his arm. *When had she taken off her gloves?* He swallowed a groan at the sensation of skin upon skin. "I heard about the unfortunate mishap of her first Season, but I never learned the name of the gentleman. I'm sorry he came here this week in his father's place."

He stared at her hand, noting the absence of a ring, the

slender fingers on his cuff, wishing he could hold them there. "You had no idea I was coming either. In truth, I didn't know until yesterday morning."

"I assume you found satisfaction after the debacle?" She pressed her lips together to hide a grin. He cut the deck, she turned up the five of clubs, and the play began.

"Of course. Why do you think he blanched when he saw me?" Lucius laid down the Jack of hearts. "Ten."

"I haven't heard anything about her in years. Where did she disappear to?" She pulled the six of hearts from her cards and laid it in front of her. "Sixteen."

"At Beecham Manor, enjoying her own house party while choosing a husband." He set down the six of diamonds, making a pair. "Twenty-two for two." He moved his first peg two holes. "It seems my father is finally going to marry Lady Henning, but they both want my sister settled before the wedding."

"And how does she feel about a betrothal?" Christiana pulled out the five of spades. "Twenty-seven." She blew out a breath. "No, no, no. That look tells me you have a four."

His grin widened at her pouting lips when he laid down the four of hearts. "Thirty-one for two." He moved his second peg two holes past the first one for going out exactly on thirty-one.

They added up their cards. Lucius went first, scoring two for a run of three and four with a run of four and moved his peg six more holes. Christiana added hers along with the crib from the beginning of the game and claimed fourteen.

"Lord Beecham is a kind and caring man, so I'm happy for him." She collected the cards and passed them to Lucius.

"Like his son?"

"Which one?"

"You think you're a clever girl," he said with a chuckle. "I'm happy for him too. It may also be the only way my sister faces her fear and realizes all men outside her family are not beasts."

The deuce if he hadn't missed Christiana's banter. They could volley back and forth as quickly as a lively game of battledore and shuttlecock. Though he could think of better things to do with the racquet than hit a piece of cork with feathers in it. *Bollocks!* Now he couldn't remove the stupid smile from his face.

"Lady Annette is a wise woman. Most men are beasts." She picked up her cards and discarded two as Lucius did the same. "Though I know how she longed for a family, and marriage is the only way to attain that."

"I'll ignore part of your remark. My father's friend was there, and I have a suspicion the two of them have formed an attachment."

"How old is he?" She gave Lucius her full attention. "She must be, what, twenty-four by now?"

He nodded. "I believe Lord Weston is around forty."

"The Page brothers were the scourge of London when your sister first came out. Are they allowing these men to woo her, or must she be observed from a distance?" She drummed her fingers on the table, deciding which card to throw, a tiny smile tipping up one side of her mouth.

"We've matured." He laughed. "But you're right, we are still a wee protective."

"My father was twenty years older than my mother. They were smitten with one another until the end."

"You're right. It's not a terrible gap of years. He's young at heart, fit, and I like him."

"High praise, indeed, coming from you. How does your younger brother fare in India?" she asked, returning her attention to the cards in her hand.

"Jeremiah is married with a son. We have yet to meet the babe, but he should be coming home by Easter." He watched her fret over the next card to play and wanted to smooth the lines creasing her brow. He didn't want her to worry about anything for the rest of their lives.

"Oh, that's wonderful. Is he selling his commission?"

Lucius nodded. "Ambrose has a growing congregation, and he and Hester are expecting their first child." There were days he couldn't believe two of his younger brothers were married with families, or a babe on the way, and he had only just begun to think in that direction. Because of the woman sitting across from him.

"Time moves on, doesn't it?" she murmured. "I wanted that once. Children. Then the years went by, and… well, here I am."

"It's not too late." He leaned forward and tipped her chin up with his forefinger. "You're still young enough to carry a child if it's what you truly want."

She blinked, her eyes shining.

"Are you…?" Lucius jumped from his chair and pulled her up, crushing her body to his. "I'm so sorry. I didn't mean to make you cry." He pushed back just enough to brush a tear from her cheek, cursing himself for causing her distress. "I want to give you a world where there are no tears."

She sniffed. "It's not your fault. I think it's the holiday, thinking of my parents gone, how alone I am."

Without another thought, he covered her mouth with his. They clung to each other, a tangle of lips and tongue and teeth, remembering a past when they were still young. Still innocent.

With his forehead braced against hers, he whispered, "You are never alone, for I am here. I've always been here." He kissed her closed eyes, her nose, both corners of her mouth, soaking in her warmth, her sweet vanilla scent. If there was a way to stop time—now, at this very moment—he would sell his soul to do it.

"Is your brute outside the door?"

"He won't crash through it unless I scream," she said with a chuckle, then wiped her wet cheeks. "Shall we finish the game?"

It was as if their kiss had removed the wall between them. Lucius had been tense with the sexual tension between them, wondering if she would allow him to touch her again, if he would lose his mind if she didn't. The rest of the game was full of laughter, recounting memories, and telling her of his family. He was at his most charming, and she was as witty and amusing as he remembered.

"I don't believe I've felt so much like myself in years," she said as she pegged out. "It's as if the young Christiana has returned for Christmas."

"A Christmas miracle. You're welcome."

Her smile melted his heart, a puddle swishing around in his chest.

***

His charm, sincerity combined with humor, was burrowing under her skin. How could she have forgotten how magnetic he was? As if she had no choice but to be near him.

Yet, she had let Edward overshadow that attraction for a few brief weeks while Lucius had been away. Long enough to convince an innocent girl to marry him, to believe it was Lucius who was the rogue in disguise. A young man tasting of freedom. Edward had explained it was all an act to deceive her, lure her into bed. Christiana had seen the Earl of Winfield as a worldly man, sophisticated compared to Lucius's practicality, droll compared to Lucius's boyish humor. Her dead husband had been a master at twisting words and situations to his advantage. And she had been the queen of fools.

As Lucius gathered the cards, she noted the tiny white

mark on the right corner of his mouth. It could have been mistaken for a dimple when he smiled. But she knew he'd received it in a mock battle with his brothers, an oak branch whittled to a sharp point and used as a sword.

They had a history together. Their families were acquainted, though she and Lucius hadn't met formally until she was sixteen. Her mother had wanted her to wait for her first Season. Christiana's father had died a year earlier, and Mama hadn't been ready to come out of mourning. But Papa would have wanted them to go on, enjoy life, she had urged her mother.

And she had met Lord Page again, his thick brown curls tamed back, gold flashing in streaks as he bowed over her hand. She thought she would be lost forever in those sea-green eyes.

"Is that a yes or a no?" he asked, bringing her back to the present.

"I beg your pardon, but I was—"

"Not listening to a word I've said? You wound me, my lady."

His smile, those pearl-white teeth, the square jaw above a strong neck—all devastating. She shivered.

"Are you cold?" He immediately stood to remove his jacket.

"No," she said, holding up her hand, palm out, as she shook her head. "I'm fine."

"Indeed."

The smile came unbidden. "You are incorrigible."

Standing before her, he held out a hand. "Shall we retire for the evening? I'm not sure what you have planned for tomorrow, but this is our second late night."

The mention of sleep brought a yawn, and she quickly covered her mouth with her hand. "I apologize. But I believe it's a sign that you are correct."

Lucius opened the door to find Jensen blocking their way. "Excuse us, I'm escorting Lady Winfield to her chambers."

"I don't think so." Jensen peered over Lucius's shoulder at her, his head tipped, eyes questioning. "My lady?"

"Yes, Mr. Jensen, you may retire now. Thank you for your service tonight."

The giant of a man nodded curtly and stepped aside. Christiana knew he would watch them from the shadows until she was safely behind a locked door.

Lucius walked her up the stairs, and she stopped at her bedroom. A thrill raced through her at the thought of him knowing where she slept. With his hands pressing against the doorway on either side of her head, he pinned her against the chamber door and bent to kiss her. A brush of lips, soft and tender, promising so much. It frightened her. And took her breath away.

Then he reached behind her, and instead of pulling her close, he opened the door. She almost fell backwards, but he caught her shoulders. "Sleep well, my little bird." Lucius walked away, his dark coat blending into the shadows.

Christiana slumped against the doorjamb. The man tugged at her soul, then brought her body to life. He was much too dangerous.

CHAPTER 8

26 December

*L*ucius tied his cravat, wishing he'd brought along his valet. But once he had convinced Wilkens to give him the invitation, he'd only wasted a moment to tell his sister where he was going. Nettie had urged him to take leave, knowing how long her brother had held a torch for Lady Winfield.

This morning, he had risen early for a hard gallop to work out some of the tension in his body. His dreams were filled with Christiana, and he had woken both mornings in a sweat. Lucius was sure they had made progress last night. He had seen flashes of the girl he'd fallen in love with. The beautiful hard shell she had used to protect herself was cracking. *Finally.*

Walking toward the dining room, he wondered what Christiana had planned for the day. At the parlor door stood the butler with his arms crossed, telling Lucius that the countess must be inside with a man. A burst of anger shot through him. Or was it jealousy?

"Who is she with?" he asked Jensen.

"Lord Frederick, sir."

Lucius couldn't hold back the sneer.

"Exactly, my lord."

"What kind of game are you playing? Do you know who my father is?"

Lucius and Jensen both lunged for the door, but the pugilist pushed his way through first. He strode across the room and stopped between Christiana and Lord Frederick.

"I suggest you adjust your tone, my lord. My butler is quite sensitive and doesn't take well to harsh tones," said Christiana with a faint smile. "To answer your question, of course I know who the Duke of Scuttleton is. Why else would you be here? Regardless of his standing, he's not entitled to take what is mine."

"I want to leave, and I will not go without that horse," hissed Lord Frederick.

"He never liked playing by the rules even as a boy." Lucius stood next to Christiana, shaking his head at Lord Frederick. "He believes they are for everyone but him."

"Shut your bloody mouth, Page." Spittle flew from Lord Frederick's mouth, his mottled face turning a deep purple above his white cravat. "My father—"

"Will be very disappointed when you return empty-handed. I would think he'd be used to it by now." Lucius didn't move when Lord Frederick lunged toward him. Jensen threw out an arm to block his progress, and the slight man fell to the ground with the small amount of resistance.

"My lord," said Christiana, rushing to his side and casting an irritated glance at both men still standing. "Are you hurt?"

"Just his pride," said Lucius, exchanging a grin with the

butler. Maybe the mammoth wasn't so bad after all. They both had Christiana's safety at heart.

Lord Frederick stood and brushed off his Clarence-blue coat. "I will have that beast if it's the last thing I do."

"Don't tease." Lucius was enjoying himself too much so early in the day.

"Lord Page, please," scolded Christiana. "Lord Frederick, why don't you have something to eat, and we'll all gather later this afternoon."

After the enraged man was gone, she turned to both men. "I appreciate being watched over, but taunting a man is beneath both of you."

"What did he offer you?" asked Lucius.

"Twice what I paid. It doesn't matter," she said with a shrug. "I'll never sell Vengeance to the duke. He and his son are both cruel to their mounts. I can't imagine his stable master or trainer being any different if they work for Scuttleton."

"Vengeance? Interesting name."

"I thought it fitting, Lord Page." She turned to Jensen. "Thank you for your help. I'll be fine for now."

Jensen bowed and left the parlor.

"Why does Scuttleton want the animal so badly?"

"From what I've learned, Vengeance is a descendant of The Godolphin Barb, a horse gifted to Louis XV from the Bay of Tuins. Barb was also mistreated and ended up a cart horse until Lord Godolphin found him and brought him to England in 1738, breeding him to produce excellent racing stock." She shrugged. "I will not let the abuse happen to his line again."

She was magnificent when her temper was up. He wanted to throw her over his shoulder and carry her up the stairs…

"Stop thinking whatever it is you are thinking," she demanded. "I know that smirk."

***

Christiana spent part of the afternoon with Lord Bentson, delivering Christmas boxes to staff and tenants. The aged man had insisted on accompanying her, and he was as entertaining with the villagers as he was with her guests. When she returned, Lady Elwood was waiting for her, her chin wobbling, brown eyes bright with excitement. "You must tell me what happened this morning. Lord Frederick stormed past me on my way to the breakfast room, muttering about difficult women and horse flesh. I said good day to him, and he yelled—yelled, mind you—that it most certainly was not a good day."

"Oh my." Christiana wondered if the man would grow tired of the contest and leave. She could only hope. "I'm sure he's calmed down. He was only upset because I wouldn't sell him the racehorse, and he's forced to stay with us longer."

"As if he's a prize himself!" Lady Elwood sniffed. "This is so much more entertaining. What is in store for us today?"

"All will be revealed when we meet in the drawing room." Christiana hurried to change, knowing the rest of her guests would soon be waiting.

"This color is so becoming on you," said Constance as she helped her mistress with the mulberry spencer, which matched her bodice, and the overdress of her pale lilac skirt. "Are you sure you'll be warm enough?"

Christiana wore several layers of petticoats, preparing for the next contest that would be outdoors. She grinned, thinking of the scheme she and the Widows League had devised.

"The guests are having a positive effect on you, my lady." Constance skillfully twisted Christiana's hair and pinned it up. "I heard you humming this morning when I came in."

"I'm…" What was she? Happy? Yes. Content? Not yet.

"Does it have anything to do with the handsome Lord

Page?" Her maid locked eyes with Christiana in the mirror as she put the finishing touches on her mistress's hair.

"It might." It did. Her mood had everything to do with him. She felt like a young girl again, but with that came the insecurities of her youth. How could he possibly want her after what she had done to him? It made no sense. Perhaps this was a plot to avenge his pride.

Don't be ridiculous.

She joined the rest of her guests in the entrance hall, having sent them word to dress warmly. Lord Bentson was laughing with Lord and Lady Elwood, Lord Frederick sulked near the door, and Lord Page was outside, speaking with her butler.

Constance followed her with her fur-lined cape. "Are we ready?" Christiana asked the group. They nodded or murmured they were. "Excellent. Shall we?" She led the way outside to a closed sleigh.

The Elwoods climbed in, followed by Lord Bentson and Lord Frederick. She looked to Lucius, who shook his head. "There is nothing you could do—well, almost nothing—to convince me to be trapped inside a conveyance with that imbecile. I will follow on horseback."

She envied him, especially when she realized she'd have to sit next to Lord Frederick. "Very well." As Lucius helped her up the steps, Christiana saw Lord Bentson scoot closer to Lord Frederick and pat the empty seat beside him with a wink.

"You dear man," she murmured as she eased onto the velvet squab. "I could give you a point just for your chivalry."

"Not to worry, my dear. An old man like myself has learned to sense certain things." His thick gray brows wiggled up and down. "Your gratitude could always include an extra point."

She laughed. As the pair of black coach horses sped across

the snow-covered ground, she listened to the Elwoods speak of their children and grandchildren. Christiana realized Lord Elwood was much more congenial than she'd thought. He obviously doted on his wife—something she never would have guessed from their previous meetings. He laughed heartily at something she said, and Christiana wondered if they had been a love match or if their affection had grown over the years.

Bells jingled to the rhythm of the horses' trotting pace. The landscape sped by, glossy white fields, great oaks without their leaves, the bare branches seeming to reach for some unseen object. Pine trees added color to the bare woods. She saw a hare dash out from its burrow and duck back inside. The sleigh came to a stop. The group stood before five large sections of tree trunks, each with a rope secured to it.

"The winner of the contest will be the one who moves his slice of tree trunk the farthest," she announced. "They are all approximately the same shape and weight, so no one is at a disadvantage."

"A contest of strength?" asked Lucius, his eyes gleaming as if he'd already won.

"I didn't say that." Christiana assumed the men would think so.

"You expect *me* to pull a piece of wood *by hand*?" Lord Frederick asked.

"However you think best," said Christiana.

"I will not."

"Do you forfeit?" asked Lucius, nodding and smiling at the same time.

"*No!*"

"You could use your card and pass on this challenge," reminded Christiana.

"I believe I will," said Lord Bentson. "Use the card, not forfeit."

"I understand," agreed Christiana.

Lord Elwood picked up the rope first and moved it fifty feet before stopping to catch his breath. "Do I get another try?"

"As long as you hold the rope, you may continue," explained Christiana. "We have until dark."

Lord Frederick grunted and moaned, pulling on his trunk and moving it a foot. "This is ridiculous. I call foul."

"On who?" asked an amused Lord Page. He walked over to the panting man, stood next to him, and pointed to the distant house. "Pretend your father is at the house. He has your allowance, and if you don't get there quickly, he will give it to Jensen, the butler."

"You think you're so clever. Let's see how far you can pull the bloody log." Lord Frederick sat down on his piece of wood.

Christiana saw Lord Elwood had pulled his log another fifty feet and was panting heavily. She didn't want anyone to have an apoplexy.

"Elwood, dear, either rest or stop there," called his wife. "Do you want me to help?"

Lord Elwood rolled his eyes but stopped. "I'll be fine, my sweet. Just need to catch my breath."

Lord Page picked up his rope and began pulling the slice of trunk. Even through his greatcoat, Christiana could see the muscular form straining as he passed Lord Elwood in one try. This got Lord Frederick up, and he managed ten more feet before whining about the cold and ruining his gloves.

Within an hour, the flask of buttered rum was passed around. Lady Elwood, Lord Bentson, and Christiana serenaded the log pullers with "I Saw Three Ships Come Sailing In" and "The First Noel" to keep spirits up. When all three men had declared they were done, Lucius had gone the farthest.

"I believe I claim the next point," he said, rubbing his hands.

"*So* unexpected," mumbled Lord Frederick.

Christiana shook her head. "I have not taken my turn."

The entire group looked at her as if she'd grown horns. She was looking forward to this. "Shall we return to the house? I'm famished."

Everyone agreed. "But Lady Winfield, you just said you hadn't taken your turn," reminded Lord Bentson.

Christiana spoke to the driver, who backed the sleigh up to the last round of wood. She picked up the rope, sat on the iron ledge at the back of the sleigh, and called to her guests. "I'm ready."

"Wh-what are you doing?" cried Lord Frederick. "That's cheating!"

Lord Bentson slapped his knee. "'Pon my soul," he said, laughing. "She didn't cheat, just outsmarted us."

CHAPTER 9

ONCE UPON A WINDOW©

Midnight in the library

*L*ucius waited, leaning against the hearth of the library, listening to the crackle of the fire. His toe tapped a light *thump* in the thick wool of the Axminster carpet. He studied the miniatures on the mantel. Christiana's parents, her grandparents, saw the resemblance between the women. He yanked on the bottle-green waistcoat that matched his coat, tugged at his cravat, then brushed an imaginary speck off his white trousers. He paced before the floor-length windows, their heavy draperies like hulking guards, blocking the cold from the frosted panes, then perused the selection of old tomes on the bookshelves.

The score so far was tied between Lord Bentson, Christiana, and himself. He led the midnight challenge one to zero. Since today's challenge had been one of wit, he would do the same. A challenge of their minds. He smiled, knowing this point would probably go to her.

"Good evening, Lord Page."

Her sultry voice swirled around him, tugging at his heart, warming his soul. Lucius knew she was interested, tempted, but he didn't know if she was ready to marry him. And that *must* be the end result. The only logical conclusion for the two of them. He understood her hesitation. Edward had lured her, laying his trap carefully.

Lucius hadn't realized how malicious his friend truly was until then. Their confrontation before the wedding had been ugly, and the men had never spoken to each other again. It had broken Lucius's heart to know Christiana would be held under the man's thumb, never pampered and adored as she deserved, only used as a tool of vengeance. How had he not seen Edward's hatred earlier? It had burned so brightly after university, smoldering during their friendship until the flames of opportunity set the torch on fire.

He rose and offered his arm, which she took. "You didn't tell me how it went today? Are your tenants well? Did they enjoy the boxes you delivered?"

Christiana nodded. She was lovely in a simple muslin gown of pale blue, the same color as her eyes. Her honey-blonde hair was twisted in the back and fell in long curls to fall across her shoulders. He wanted to trace the cord on the side of her long, slender neck with a finger and follow that with his lips.

"Everyone is healthy and grateful for the gifts." She beamed. "It's one of my favorite days of the year. A few hours when I can join the villagers, sit with them, and talk of crops and babies and the coming spring. I often feel as if I have more in common with my tenants than I do those I left behind in London."

"You probably do. Honesty, integrity… traits that the common man cherishes and many of the peers value only when it suits them." He poured them both a glass of madeira, and they settled before the cheerful fire, its flickering light casting long shadows across the room. The wingback chairs were made of a buttery-soft leather, and he tipped his head back with a sigh.

"May I ask you a question?"

His heart pounded. What did she want to know? "Of course," was all he said, silently ordering his pulse to stop racing.

"Did you think I cheated this afternoon?"

He shook his head. "You didn't give any specific instructions. In fact, when Lord Frederick asked if you expected him to pull it by hand, your answer was whatever he thought best. That was clever."

"Thank you." Her smile could have lit the darkest corner of the library. "What impish game do you have planned for tonight?"

"Again, I shall follow your lead. A game of wits, challenging one another with riddles. The first to make five points wins."

"I see. Who shall go first?"

"I will give you preference," he said with a wink.

"Since I did not know the game in advance, you may go first."

"Fine. Let me think." He drummed his fingers on his thigh. "What is always in front of you but can never be seen?"

Christiana pursed her lips in thought, then laughed. "The future. Heaven knows, my life would be different if I could have seen it!"

"And mine, too, no doubt." His heart twisted a little when her smile faded. He wanted happiness shining in her eyes again. "Your turn."

She tapped her forefinger against her chin. "Hmm. I know. What has hands but cannot clap?"

"A clock. I'm expecting you to challenge me, not humor

me." Lucius drummed his fingers again on his leg. "What is at the end of a rainbow?"

Christiana rolled her blue eyes. "It's a pot of—" She closed her mouth abruptly and shook her head. "Too easy… a W!"

He laughed and nodded. "I knew you would get it. Two-one."

"I cannot talk, but I always reply when spoken to."

He studied her profile while he ran through the possibilities, but his thoughts got caught up in her perfectly shaped earlobe, nibbling at it with his teeth…

"Have I stumped you?" she asked, one brow arched.

"Do you know how distracting your ear can be?" he countered.

"Mine in particular, or ears in general? This isn't a riddle out of turn, is it?" One corner of her mouth quirked up in a half smile.

"No," he said with a chuckle, "and just yours, my sweet bird." Lucius loved how her blush began on her neck and climbed slowly to her cheeks. "My answer is one's conscience."

"A very good guess, and one which might work for you but not everyone." She gave him a quick side-glance. "We both know too many people without one."

Were they thinking of the same person?

"Cannot talk, but always replies when spoken to," he murmured, racking his brain for another response. "May I have a hint?"

"You'll forfeit your point," she said with a smirk.

"Doesn't matter, it's driving me mad. And my pride won't allow you to just give me the answer." He crossed his arms over his chest, waiting.

"Think of being in a cave." She grinned. "And calling for me."

That definitely set his imagination in motion but didn't

help him with the riddle. His fingers began drumming again, and he turned his attention to the crackling flames. "An echo!" he shouted with glee.

Christiana clapped her hands. "Well done! But it's still two-one in my favor."

"Now, let's see…" He snapped his fingers. "What has teeth but cannot bite?"

"Papa's old hunting dog," she said, giggling. "No, seriously, a comb?"

"You haven't lost your sense of humor, I see." He was glad of it. "Three-one. I'm not doing so well. I'll have to think of something harder."

She took a sip of wine, crossed her legs, and rested the glass on top of her knee. "What is always on its way but never arrives?"

"Ha! Tomorrow!" He hit the arm of the chair with his fist, grinning back when she gave a huff at his speedy retort. "Three-two. I'm catching up. Now I must stump you, so I have a chance to tie."

Christiana placed her glass on the table between him, tucked her feet underneath her, and leaned on the side of the chair with her chin resting on her fist. It felt so right—the two of them sitting together before the fire, chatting the evening away as any married couple might do. It was what he wanted, needed, longed for. And she was within his grasp.

"There are four men on horseback stopped at a cross-roads, each going in a different direction. When they all continue their journey, none of them cross paths. How is that possible?"

Christiana closed her eyes, one foot tapping against the arm of the chair as she thought. Once she shook her head, as if eliminating a possibility. "They all turned to the right."

"Bravo!" He clapped. "Four-two."

"Why do you still give me a token every November?" she

asked, eyes drawn to her skirt as she smoothed the material over her knees.

"Because it's the month you were born," he answered cautiously, wondering what her point might be.

"Even after I treated you abhorrently, you can still send me tokens of affection?" Her gaze strayed to the curio cabinet near the hearth.

He could see a few larger objects—vases, he assumed by the shape—and a collection of smaller figures. Were his gifts in there? "Christiana, you weren't alone in his duplicity. He fooled me too. I had no idea how much…" He needed to choose his words carefully.

"He hated you?" she supplied. Her blue eyes locked with his. "He did, you know. Hated that you had a wonderful family, siblings who watched out for one another. Parents who loved you."

He nodded. "I know that now. He spat it out, like venom from a hissing snake, the night before your wedding. He considered you the ultimate triumph over me. But I never understood why."

"Edward was the only surviving child, the heir to the earl-dom. The pressure on him just to survive was tremendous. His father oversaw every detail of his life once his older brothers had died." She took a sip of wine, then continued, "There was no civility between his parents, let alone love. He was raised by servants. His father only attended him to give orders and reprimand him for doing something not up to expectations."

"He told me once he hated his father, then laughed. I assumed they'd had an argument as all fathers and sons do." Lucius knew he was fortunate growing up in a loving family. "But what does that have to do with me?"

"Everything came so easy for you. Your studies, your confidence. You were excellent in sporting and games, mastering anything you attempted." She finished her madeira and set the glass down. "Edward, for all his bravado, wasn't academically inclined. He was berated for subpar grades, was only passable at riding, marksmanship, fencing. He had to work hard to be mediocre at the things you excelled in with little effort. So, he won the item he thought you prized above all else."

"You." Lucius was stunned. He had thought Edward simply wanted what he couldn't have, a spoiled boy who demanded everyone's toys. But this had been personal. "He almost ruined our lives because he was jealous?"

Christiana nodded, then stood. She walked to the cabinet and opened the door on the right side, reaching in to touch an object with a fingertip. "Why do you say *almost* ruined our lives?"

"He's dead and can't hurt us anymore. We're here together, and his treachery will never keep us apart again unless…"

"Unless I refuse?" She took out a small porcelain robin from the case. "You sent me this when Mama died. My grandmother used to tell me that when a robin appeared it was a messenger from someone beloved who had passed. To let those who still remained know they were at peace."

Lucius rose and joined her, peering in the dark cabinet and recognizing several of the figurines he had sent her over the years. "My mother told me the same folktale. I thought of it when your mother died and hoped it would give you comfort, even though I could not."

"It did—it does—more than you know. When she died, I was sitting in her bedroom, crying in a heap on the rug. I looked up to see a robin perched outside the window. I was sure it was Mama. I went back every morning for a week to watch the bird. And then it was gone. It seemed as if I had lost her all over again." She looked up at him with glistening eyes. "Then your gift arrived. It brought me light in my darkest hours."

"I'm glad." A giant vise locked around Lucius's heart and squeezed. To think of the pain she had gone through, alone, knowing she was truly without any family. He couldn't imagine the emptiness.

"It was a very thoughtful gift, Lucius. Something a dear friend would give to another dear friend."

"You are more than that to me," he whispered in her ear. "I want you to be my world, to let my life revolve around you, loving you, protecting you, making you happy again."

He gently took the robin from her and placed it back on the shelf. Cupping her neck with one hand, his thumb stroking her jaw, he pulled her close with his free arm. "We need to leave the past behind us and look to our future. For we have one, my sweet bird, if you'll only let it be."

Her lips were soft and warm and inviting. He accepted her offer and traced the seam of her mouth with his tongue, asking for entrance. Her lips parted, and he swept in, tasting the sweet red wine, feeling her hands move around his neck, her fingers threading through his hair. He groaned as she yielded and pressed against him, giving in, giving him hope. Giving him strength to never let her go.

When he ended the kiss, her head fell against his chest, her breath coming in pants. "Your parents would want you to be with a man who makes you happy and feel safe. I believe I'm that man."

"You make me doubt everything I've known to be true for so many years: Most men are beasts. One of the few who isn't, after I abused him and am no longer worthy of his attention, still wants me. So forgiveness—even of myself—is possible." She blinked up at him, shook her head, as if dispelling a cloud surrounding it. "But it can't be that simple, especially the latter."

"Love *is* that simple. We are the complication." He brushed a tear from her cheek with a thumb. "I can forgive you for being naïve and listening to a skilled liar. I can forgive myself for being more boy than man, for not fighting for you as I should have. We've both made mistakes, but staying apart would only be a worse blunder."

Christiana took in a shaky breath, her palms sliding down his chest. "I'm afraid you have turned me into some kind of martyr, set me high on an unsteady pedestal. A year from now, two years from now, you may wake up one morning and realize I'm not the woman you remember. I'm just a weak, foolish countess who doesn't deserve such attention."

He barked a laugh. He couldn't help it. "Never. I'm not seeing you or the world through some magic lens, creating a fantasy which doesn't exist. I love you with all your imperfections. And I pray you can look past mine."

With a half sigh, half moan, Christina pushed away from him. "You give me much to think about."

"That means I'm on your mind." He waggled his brows.

When she reached the door, Christiana turned. "What can be touched but never seen?"

He looked at her and responded without hesitation, "My heart."

"And mine."

His expression sobered as she left the room, the hulking shadow of the butler following her. Had she just hinted that he'd touched her heart?

Christiana was a complex woman. She was dedicated to her tenants and the villagers and cared about their welfare. She had the courage to help other women find retribution. Yet, she wasn't brave enough to forgive herself. For if she did, she'd be vulnerable to being hurt again. And like him, neither could survive another heartbreak.

CHAPTER 10

27 December

*C*hristiana woke to a splendid day. The sun shone brightly, the layer of snow glistening across the lawn, tiny icicles clinging to the branches, sending a shimmery spray into the air with each light breeze. Every day with Lucius seemed to lift a bit more of the burden from her shoulders, lightening her load and her mood. Now, her first inclination was not always negative or doubting another's sincerity. Perhaps with time, her once optimistic self would return permanently. If…

Her stomach rumbled, and she scooped an extra egg onto her plate. Lord and Lady Elwood sat across from her, and Lord Bentson sat on her right. Lord Frederick was either sleeping late or having his breakfast in his room, which suited the rest of the guests who were tired of his incessant whining.

"Shall we dress for the outdoors again, Lady Winfield?" asked Lord Bentson.

"Since the weather is being cooperative, yes." Christiana returned to her seat next to the elderly man. "Shall I tell you what the contest will be?"

"Oh, yes."

"Please."

"Of course," they all said at once.

"Archery."

"Excellent. I'm quite proficient with a bow," said Lucius from the doorway.

Christiana's heart jumped at the sound of his voice. She waited while he filled a plate and joined them. Her mind went back to the night before. Kisses at midnight were becoming part of her nightly ritual. How would she feel when he left? Would she miss their rendezvous? Return to the cynical woman she'd become?

"That color brings out the blush of your cheeks," he said softly as he walked by.

"Thank you, Lord Page," she murmured, the wings in her stomach taking flight as she looked down at her pale-rose day dress. Delicate white lace trimmed the muslin collar and cuffs. "Did you go out this morning?"

He nodded. "I like starting the day with a ride. Gets my blood moving, lets my brain wake up slowly with the rising sun."

"You make a frigid hour on horseback sound poetic," said Lady Elwood with a laugh. "I hope the archery contest is nearby."

"She looked like a giant onion peeling off all those layers," added her husband.

"Elwood, mind your tongue!" his wife scolded, her round face turning pink.

Christiana bit her lip, trying not to grin at the married

couple's teasing. "No, it will be on the back lawn. If you prefer, ma'am, you could watch from inside."

"Wonderful," agreed Lady Elwood. "My husband is known for his skill in the hunt. A target should be no trouble at all, eh, my lord?" She popped her elbow in the man's side.

"This is the day I gain a point." Lord Elwood clapped his hands and stood, his dark-brown eyes shining with anticipation. "I shall send for my own bow right away."

***

The group gathered on the lawn, their breath shimmering in the frosty air. It was a quiet afternoon, their boots crunching on the snow as they walked toward the target. The green boughs around them bent with a layer of white. The men wore heavy greatcoats, and Christiana had on her long, deep-blue spencer rather than the cumbersome cloak of yesterday. Her fur muff had been replaced with leather gloves.

Lord Frederick was sullen, as usual, complaining he was better at fencing. "You are setting me up to fail," he accused Christiana.

"How could she possibly know you were coming in your father's stead? And even if she did, how would she know your strengths and weaknesses?" asked Lord Page, a frown marring his handsome face. "Stop making excuses for your incompetence."

Christiana glanced over her shoulder to see Lady Elwood waving enthusiastically from the window. She was becoming fast friends with the older woman. It wasn't only the maternal side of the viscountess that drew Christiana, but the woman's forthright attitude. She had no difficulty stating her mind, and Christiana found she trusted Lady Elwood. Something which rarely happened so quickly.

The men chose their bows, nocking arrows to the string and testing the resistance. Lord Elwood beamed, as if he already knew the outcome. This wasn't Christiana's favorite activity, but she had passable skill. By the way Lord Frederick was holding his bow, she knew she could beat him.

"I shall begin," she said, taking her place on the mark and sucking a chilly breath. She nocked her arrow and pulled back, feeling the balance before letting loose.

Whoosh! Not center, but along the edge. Better than she had hoped for. The men clapped, and she took a bow. "Lord Page? Would you like to go next?"

He nodded, focusing his emerald-green eyes on the target. *Whoosh*. His arrow landed in the center circle but close to her own. Lucius peered over his shoulder and winked at her. Was he losing on purpose? No, she decided, he was too competitive and wanted to defeat the duke's son.

"Good shot," said Lord Bentson, squinting his eyes at the target.

"Lord Frederick?" She noted the man was still pouting as he trudged to the mark, like a little boy being dragged for a bath. When his arrow landed far from the center, she understood his reluctance. Was the man good at anything but complaining?

"I hate this game," he mumbled, shoulders drooping. "I call for a drinking game."

"I'll go next," announced Lord Elwood. His grin fell away as he nocked his arrow, concentrated on the wafer, and let loose. *Whoosh*. Almost dead center. "That's the way it's done!"

"Very impressive, sir," said Lucius. "This may indeed be your day. Lord Bentson, I believe it's your turn."

The elderly man gave a nod and walked to the mark. "It's been a while since I've done this, but in my day…" His bent fingers nocked the arrow, and he lifted the bow, aiming at the target. *Whoosh*. The arrow hit dead center, quivering against Lord Elwood's.

Silence reigned while every mouth fell open except for Bentson.

"My lord, well done!" said Lord Page, finding his voice first.

"It's a fluke. I say we go another round," huffed Lord Elwood. "I won't be beaten by an old man."

Lord Bentson chuckled. "I'm game if the rest of you are."

Christiana shook her head. "You may continue if you like," she told the group, "but the point goes to Lord Bentson." Men were such vain creatures, she'd decided. Even her Lucius. *Her Lucius.* How had that niggled its way into her brain?

Lord Bentson bowed. "Thank you, my lady."

"I must admit I'm surprised. What other secrets are you hiding?" She studied the old man's face, seeing him in a new light. He was growing on her, becoming more than an acquaintance.

"You may find out one day." He gave her a wink, nocked another arrow, and sent it flying to join his first arrow, dead center. "Fluke indeed," he mumbled.

***

Lady Elwood patted her husband's hand. "You won at piquet tonight, my dear. You are still my champion."

Her husband grunted and held up his glass. "To my wife, who always finds the brightness on a gloomy day."

They all raised their glasses. "To our hostess, who has provided a most unique and entertaining house party," added Lord Bentson. "Your mother would be proud."

Christiana paused in taking a sip of her wine. "Did you know my mother well?" she asked. "Besides the correspondence concerning the vase."

The older man nodded. "That's a story for another time."

"It's too early to retire," said Lord Elwood. "Anyone up for a game of billiards? Page, are you feeling lucky?"

Christiana recognized the challenge in his voice. Exactly the tone needed to prod Lucius into playing. But when they all rose to watch the game, Lord Bentson remained seated.

"I thought I'd sit here and enjoy my brandy and the fire," he said apologetically to his hostess. "The old bones tire more easily as the years fly by."

"Then I shall sit with you," she declared, pouring herself another glass of wine and taking the wingback chair next to him.

After the other guests had left, she could not contain her curiosity any longer. "So, tell me the story of how you knew my mother."

Bentson smiled. "We met during her first Season. She was a beauty." His eyes grew distant, as if he found himself back in a ballroom decades ago. "She was standing by a wall, hoping not to be noticed. I believe she had spilled some punch on her dress and was trying to hide it until she could leave or find her shawl."

"Mama was always a bit clumsy. She often said she wore more food than she ate," Christiana agreed. "An exaggeration of course. She never minded making fun of herself."

"There wasn't an arrogant bone in her body," murmured Lord Benston, still staring into the fire. "She wasn't clumsy on the dance floor. I wish the waltz had been introduced back then."

"You enjoy dancing?"

He nodded. "Once upon a time with the right partner. And I believed she was."

"You… you were in love with my mother?" The conversation had taken an unexpected turn. "What happened?"

"I was young and foolish, craving adventure. Love was secondary to working for the Crown, playing spy, courting danger." The old man shook his head. "By the time I was ready to settle down, your mother was married. According to the on-dits, it had been a love match."

Christiana nodded, smiling. "They were very happy. And you?"

"My wife was a lovely woman. A good mother, kind, excellent at managing a household." He studied the brandy, his knobby fingers gripping the crystal glass. "I was lucky. I was content. But still, I always wondered…"

"About Mama?" Her mind raced to remember any mention of this man before the letters began asking to purchase the vase. Had her mother cared for him once? Or had she continued to carry a torch for him, even though she was happy with Papa, also wondering what might have been?

"When I heard your father died, I wrote to her under the guise of offering my condolences and wanting to buy the Ming vase." He chortled. "I needed to know if she hated me for leaving, not asking her to marry me, or if she had been truly happy. I was an arrogant young man to think she would wait."

"Did you find out?" Her heart went out to this man. She understood unrequited love all too well.

"No, she did not hate me. Yes, she had been truly happy."

"But she wouldn't sell you the vase. Why?" The piece of porcelain had been in the curio cabinet for as long as she could remember. It must have been one of Mama's favorites.

"It became a ruse for our letters. An excuse to touch one another's lives again. It wasn't the antique I wanted so badly as it was her attention." He took a drink of the brandy, then let out a loud sigh. "I found the piece during a mission early in my career, before she was married. I sent it to her with a note, comparing the priceless object to her beauty."

"You're a romantic." She was surprised to learn Mama had kept a gift from another man throughout her marriage. "Do you want the vase as a reminder of my mother?"

He nodded, his hazel eyes glistening. "Ridiculous, I know. But having that piece in my own library, where I can touch it each day, knowing she had done the same, would give me comfort in my last years."

Christiana went on her knees before the elderly man and took his gnarled hand in hers. "Lord Bentson, I had no idea the sentimental value attached to the vase."

"It's why I hope to win the next contest." He removed his hand from hers and patted her cheek. "It gives me solace that you know our secret, and it didn't turn you away from me."

"It doesn't matter who wins," she disagreed. "With this knowledge, you have become a link to my past. Another voice who can share my love for her and my sorrow for her loss."

"Lady Winfield, walking away from your mother was the biggest mistake of my life. When one finds the love of his lifetime, he should snatch it and hold tight, never let it go." He gave her a sad smile. "Promise you won't make the same mistake I did."

Voices echoed in the hall. Christiana stood, smoothing her skirts as she returned to her chair, thinking on Lord Bentson's words. Her guests spilled into the room.

"Lord Page beat me again," announced Lord Elwood. "But I massacred Lord Frederick."

"Where is he?" asked Christiana, not seeing the duke's son with the others.

"He's nursing his pride with a bottle of whisky in his chamber," answered Lady Elwood. "That boy is monstrous spoiled."

"Good riddance," said Lucius, tossing a knee-weakening smile at Christiana.

"The score now stands Bentson two, Lady Winfield one, and Lord Page one." Lady Elwood narrowed her eyes at Lord Bentson. "You have become the man to beat, my lord."

"We'll have to see what's in store for us tomorrow," said the older earl. "I know from experience how luck can desert a man as quickly as it favors him."

CHAPTER 11

28 December

*L*ucius woke early. The previous night, during his private archery session with Christiana, he had gained him another point. Two-one in his favor. While he wanted to win the daily challenge for Charles Wilkens and his uncle, to thank them for this opportunity with Christiana, the midnight contests were the most important. If he won, it gave him more time to woo the woman, to convince her that destiny had brought them back together.

He wrapped his greatcoat around him, the wind whipping up tiny snow swirls that wrapped around his boots as they crunched through the thin layer of snow. A storm was brewing; he could feel it in his bones. *The devil if I don't sound like my father.*

The dim light coming from the stable window didn't surprise him. The youngest stable boy had picked up on

Lucius's habit and met him now with his horse, Boots, ready for a morning ride. Of course, the lad received a coin for his trouble. But Lucius appreciated the boy's ambition.

This morning, he was met with a saddled horse and a tear-streaked face. "What is the matter? Are you hurt?"

"One o' the guests said to saddle Vengeance, said he had to try the horse out 'fore he bought it," sniffed the redheaded boy, his freckles shiny on his wet cheeks. "I tol' 'im no one could ride Vengeance without milady's permission. If he would jus' wait until the sun come up, the stable master would speak wi' her."

"You did the right thing," soothed Lucius. "Did he hurt you?"

The lad shook his head. "He ordered me to fetch the saddle and bridle for when the stable master came. And when it was found I 'ad denied a lord, he said I'd be beaten. So I did as I was tol' and then he sent me back into the tack room. That's when he locked me in."

"He what?"

The boy nodded. "He locked me in, saddled Vengeance, and took 'im."

Lucius swore under his breath, not wanting to alarm the lad. "How did you get out?"

"I climbed out the window, but he was gone. So, I readied yer mount, knowin' ye'd be here shortly."

Lucius tousled the stable boy's hair. "You did exactly as I would have done. What direction did he take and how much of a lead does he have?"

"South toward London and the village, about fifteen minutes ago, milord," answered the boy, relief on his freckled face.

"Good. Lord Frederick isn't a man used to riding in foul weather. Fortunately, I am and so is my horse." He buttoned the top of his greatcoat, pulled up the collar, and wrapped his scarf tightly around his neck and mouth, yanking his leather gloves under his wool sleeves. "Go up to the great house and tell Cook what has happened, so she can tell Mr. Jensen, the butler. He'll know what to do."

Lucius swung onto the saddle and pulled back on the rein as his black gelding danced and pawed, feeling his owner's urgency. "With luck, I'll be back soon, leading Vengeance."

A slight kick to the flanks, and they were off. Five minutes later, the snow was coming down in heavy gusts. It whipped about his hat, filling the brim, crept down his neck, and stung his eyes. He could barely see past the puff of steam rising from Boots's nose as he pushed against the howling wind. Lucius took comfort that if his pace had slowed, so had Lord Frederick's.

It was a half hour into the village by carriage. It would take double the time in this storm. He bloody wouldn't let that cur get away with stealing a horse. *Christiana's horse.* The snow clung to his eyelashes, and he blinked to clear his vision. His fingers were going numb by the time he reached the village. He let out a sigh when he saw the lights of the small inn and tavern. If his hunch was correct, the namby-pamby had stopped here to warm up. Lucius suspected he didn't have the stamina to go far.

He dismounted in the small courtyard and walked to the stable. "Two men fool enough to be out in this weather," said a stableman, taking the reins. "Will ye be stayin'?"

Lucius shook his head. "Just until the weather clears. Where's the mount that recently came in?"

He followed the man to the back of the stable. The white stallion was quietly munching on oats. "He's a beauty, he is," said the man. "A bit small for my taste, but a high-stepper to be sure."

"He's part Arabian. You can tell by the size and this dip in his forehead," Lucius told him, pointing to the horse's fore-lock. "I'll be taking him back with me as soon as the snow quits. Find a lead rope for him and give my mount some grain while I tend to the thief. He was stolen from her estate this morning. Lady Winfield's stable master will fetch his saddle and bridle after the storm."

"Ye don't say." The man whistled. "And the fella looked to be such a gent, too. Probably stole the fine clothes besides."

Lucius pulled his hat low as he made his way to the inn. His fury was at a pitch when he slammed the door open. An older man, an apron tied around his thick body, looked up with wide eyes, then smiled. "Good morn' to ye, sir. I'll be right with ye," he said, nodding to the bowl and tankard in his hand.

Lucius scanned the public room. There were a half dozen scarred wood tables with chairs, charred ceiling beams, and a fine polished bar two locals were leaning against. Then he saw Lord Frederick, his greatcoat still covered with snow. Their gazes locked, then Lord Frederick scrambled from his chair, tripped on another, and landed face down on the worn wooden planks.

When Lucius grabbed the back of his collar and yanked the man up, he started to laugh. "Is that your nose bleeding? Did you break it yourself this time?"

Lord Frederick covered his face with his arms. "Don't touch me. I-I'll have you arrested. I'll—"

"You'll have me arrested? You stole a horse," yelled Lucius, his patience snapping. "You may be the son of a duke, but this fist belongs to the son of an earl." And he slammed it into Lord Frederick's face.

The duke's son crumpled.

The earl's son grinned.

The innkeeper moaned.

"Not to worry, he'll be gone as soon as the weather clears. Could you order a coach to take him to London? The Duke of Scuttleton will be grateful to have his boy home." Lucius tucked a boot under the unconscious man's arm and tugged up. He'd be out for a while.

"Aye, my lord. A mail coach will come through later today. I'll be sure he's on it."

The innkeeper helped Lucius pick up Lord Frederick and put him in a chair. Using the man's own scarf, he tied his hands behind the chair. "Now if he wakes, he can't cause any trouble until the coach arrives."

"Are ye hungry, my lord? Can I get ye something to eat?" asked the innkeeper, rubbing his bald head. His eyes dashed nervously back and forth between the lord before him and the one tied to the chair.

"I'd be grateful for some hot coffee or tea," Lucius replied as he removed his scarf, then his greatcoat, and shook off the snow near the large hearth. The dancing flames hissed at the wet intrusions but soon sent a tingling through his hands as feeling returned. "Be at ease, my good man, for I won't leave you alone with him."

"Thank ye, milord," said the innkeeper as he backed away.

After a hot cup of tea and some warm bread with jam, Lucius was feeling much more human. Lord Frederick was stirring, and only realized he was tied up when he tried to rub his jaw... or nose or aching head. Lucius wasn't quite sure what would hurt the most.

"You blaggard, untie me!" demanded Lord Frederick.

"Not until the mail coach has arrived, and I see you on it." He finished the last sip of tea and wiped his mouth with a napkin. "What were you thinking? A duke's son turned horse thief?"

"Is my nose broken again? Why does the back of my head

hurt?" Lord Frederick mumbled. "I'll press charges against you as soon as I'm loose."

"And when I'm asked why I planted you a facer, I shall tell them you a stole horse. I can't imagine how the duke will react to that. You fell and hit your nose. It's no longer bleeding, and it doesn't look broken. I did send a deuced good right to your jaw, and when you fell backwards, you hit your head." Lucius leaned forward, his elbows on his knees. "But why did you do it?"

"I couldn't go home without the beast. She left me no choice!" screamed Lord Frederick. Then he hung his head and began to moan. "You don't understand. He's a monster."

"Who?"

"My father. He hates me, wishes I died instead of my brother. I thought this was my chance to prove…" Another moan. "He'll cut me off now, disinherit me. It's true. I can do nothing right."

"Well, if this is how you solve a problem, I'd have to agree." The actual fear on the man's face surprised Lucius. He knew the older brother had always been favored, but he hadn't known the younger one was so disliked. "And he can't disinherit you, nodcock. He can only cut you off financially. You *will* gain the title."

Lord Frederick snorted. "Little good it will do me with no blunt."

"Don't you have any of your own? No investments? No smaller estates?" He couldn't imagine still being reliant on his father for coin. "What do you do all day?"

"I'm terrible with business ventures, or so he tells me. I've always managed on my allowance, but if he quits…" Shoulders drooping, Lord Frederick breathed a loud sigh. "If I knew why he hated me so, I might be able to change his mind about me."

"Do you have any friends who could help with your

investments? Put your father off, say she's decided to keep the horse until spring. It would give you some time." Lucius frowned. Why was he helping this whiny, spiteful man? Or was it just a mask he wore to hide his pain?

Lucius had grown up in a loving household. He knew many who had not, though it didn't give them the excuse to be cruel to others. This man—and Edward—had been raised with an unloving and strict father. Both had lost their mothers, and Lucius was beginning to realize how fortunate he was. He remembered his mother, her kindness and affection. What might he have been like without that maternal love? Without a father who loved him unconditionally?

Lucius shook his head, wondering how to help the duke's son without helping him. He couldn't be disloyal to his sister, who this man had ruined. He couldn't betray Christiana by not returning with Vengeance.

"I think the time has come for you to become a man and stand on your own," Lucius finally said, running a hand through his hair. "Have you ever asked your father why he treats you as he does? Perhaps it is your insecurities he hates so much. Have you ever asked your father for help in business matters?"

Lord Frederick stared at him as if he had two heads.

"Well?"

"No. I-I didn't think he would give me an answer. Or I wouldn't like what I heard."

"So, a moment of truth is worse than this?" Lucius flung out his arm, indicating the man tied to a chair and the stable beyond. "Can you imagine what the broadsheets would do with an incident like this?"

"Crucify me as they did your sister." Lord Frederick threw his head back and closed his eyes. "My life is a catastrophe."

"Then fix it. Use your allowance for investments. Start

slow, see what works, invest more. Hire a man to help you if you have no friends." Lucius slapped his forehead with his palm. "You're a duke's son! Use your connections, use the title that will be yours someday, and be your own man. Before you become the Duke of Scuttleton."

"You make it sound easy."

"Ha! Nothing worthwhile is easy. Those who make it look effortless are working hard behind closed doors." Lucius untied the man's hands, confident Lord Frederick wouldn't be able to do any more harm. Today, anyway. "Grow up. People don't like Frederick the boy. But they may like Frederick the man. Find out who he is and take control of your own life."

Lord Frederick rubbed his wrists and gave Lucius a side-glance. "I *want* to do better."

"Then do it."

"I suppose you'll tell everyone what happened here?" Lord Frederick's pale-blue eyes pleaded. "I'll never have the opportunity to right the wrongs I've done if they get wind of this in Town."

Lucius shook his head. Against his better judgment, he would show mercy. It was what his sister would want him to do. Maybe. Probably. "I'll have to tell Lady Winfield, but she's no gossip. We can keep it between us. If anyone asks, we'll call it a misunderstanding."

"Thank you, Lord Page." Lord Frederick stood and offered his hand. "You are kinder than I deserve."

"Don't make me regret it." The snow had stopped. Lucius tossed some coins on the rough wooden table and put on his greatcoat. "What will you do?"

"Take your advice. Father isn't expecting me until after Twelfth Night, so I may call upon some friends as you mentioned. Perhaps have a plan before I go home." His eyes held regret. "I didn't mean for that fiasco to happen with your sister. She didn't deserve the notoriety I forced upon her."

"You're apologizing to the wrong person," Lucius said, tugging on his hat. "Though if you do make amends with my sister, I suggest keeping your distance. Her right punch has only gotten stronger."

CHAPTER 12

*C*hristiana sat by the parlor room window, looking out onto the drive. On any other day, she would enjoy the pristine white covering the drive and front lawn. But today, the weather only brought uneasiness because Lord Page was somewhere battling the gusty winds. Her nails bit into the palms of her hands as every terrible scenario went through her head. Lucius in a snowdrift with broken bones. Lucius knocked unconscious by Lord Frederick. *Well, that may be farfetched.* Lucius shot by Lord Frederick. She was still in shock after learning Lord Frederick had stolen Vengeance and prayed the horse would soon be home. Truly, they couldn't have gotten farther than the village with the incoming storm.

A tiny dark form appeared in the distance between the trees lining the drive. As it drew near, she could see two horses. Lord Page's black gelding and the white stallion. There was no rider on Vengeance. Had Lucius killed the duke's son? Her hand flew to her mouth before she scolded herself. No, of course he hadn't.

She pulled the bell, then instructed the maid to fetch her

mantle. Minutes later, she was walking down the portico steps to meet Lord Page.

"My kingdom for a horse," she cried out as he came within earshot. A gust tugged at her hood, and tiny icicles flew from the overhead branches, biting her cheeks. Above, puffy gray clouds threatened more snow, but she no longer cared. Lucius had returned the hero. Relief came off her like a wet woolen cloak.

"And I was looking for a kingdom. How fortuitous," Lucius answered, his smile warming her, though his nose was red as a baked apple.

Christiana grasped Vengeance by the halter and stroked his long nose, murmuring softly to him. "I promised you no harm would come to you again, though it wasn't my doing this time."

The stable boy and stable master, Jack, met them in the courtyard. "Ye got 'im, milord," said the boy. "Did he get far?"

Lucius shook his head. "Only to the local inn. We waited out the storm and went our separate ways." He caught the eye of the stable master. "It was a... misunderstanding if anyone was to ask."

Jack nodded and took the lead and rein of both horses.

"I left the saddle and bridle behind. Could someone fetch it on their next trip to the village?"

"Aye, sir," said Jack. "He looks no worse for the wear, milady. 'Tis a blessing, to be sure."

Christiana had to agree. She tucked her arm through Lord Page's as they returned to the house. "Are you hungry?"

"I am. The innkeeper provided tea and some fresh bread, but the ride has made me ravenous."

They joined the others in the breakfast room. Christiana poured coffee for Lucius herself while he filled a plate from the side table. They told the other guests that Lord Frederick had been called away and bid them all a happy holiday.

Lord Elwood snorted. "I can't see the boy being *happy* about anything."

"He's not a boy, my dear. He's a man," corrected his wife.

"Then he should act like one," her husband grumbled.

"So, it's down to the three of us," said Lord Bentson. "I only need one more win." His smile deepened the creases in his face and neck, and as Christiana watched him slap his knee, she made a decision.

He would get the vase regardless of the points. The old man, her mother's first love, had become a friend. She wanted to make Lord Bentson happy, and at the same time, in an odd way, make Mama happy too.

"Lady Winfield?"

Christiana blinked, realizing she had missed part of the conversation. "I'm sorry. My mind was wandering. Were you wondering about the contest today?"

Everyone nodded.

"Marksmanship with pistols."

"Ooh," whispered Lady Elwood. "My dear, this could be your time."

"I'm almost as good at pistols," said Lord Bentson. "This could be *my* time!"

They all turned to stare at Lord Page. He shrugged and winked at Christiana. "It depends on the day."

The weather cleared, though heavy dark clouds still hung low in the sky. Once again, Christiana and the gentlemen went out on the back lawn, waving at Lady Elwood through the window. Her bright red dress and turban were easily identified even at a distance. A footman had tacked a thin, round wafer of paper to a tree, and she carried three replacements.

"Whoever hits the center circle gains three points. Any other hits are worth one. You may choose a different pistol for each of your three tries or use the same one. Mr. Jensen will reload for us." She opened the three boxes containing both single and double-barrel pistols and then indicated two rifles. "There should be something here for everyone."

Lord Bentson was true to his word. He landed one shot in the bull's eye and two more just outside with a single-barrel pistol, giving him five points. Lord Elwood chose the rifle, being his weapon of choice for hunting. He made the bull's-eye twice with the third shot landing outside the center. "Seven," he bellowed. "Puts me in the lead."

Lucius also made the bull's-eye twice, but his third shot was just on the border of the center circle, tying with Elwood. Christiana missed her first shot completely, hitting the tree trunk above, and then finished with two decent shots near the center for two points.

After examining the wafers, it was decided Lord Page's final shot was closer to the bull's-eye than Lord Elwood's, declaring Lucius the winner.

"Demmed if you didn't beat me," said Lord Elwood good-naturedly. "Excellent marksmanship, gentlemen. I'd have you with me in a dark Cheapside alley any day."

"Thank you, my lord," said Lord Bentson. "I was known to have quite a punch in my day. It would have been a pleasure to have your back."

Christiana rolled her eyes. Men and their egos. Even this sweet old man boasted about his youthful prowess. "It seems Lord Bentson and Lord Page are tied overall with two points. But there's still time, Lord Elwood."

***

That evening, they dined on white soup, roast pheasant, and root vegetables, with a syllabub for dessert. They drank too much wine, played Hunt the Slipper—Lady Elwood had to be convinced her skirt was not an appropriate place to hide it—and sang festive songs while Christiana played the pianoforte.

As they were retiring, Lord Elwood stopped Christiana at the door. "I would like to apologize for my pompous introduction when we first met. It was wrong of me to assume the use of your woods. It was worse when I also assumed you should then sell it to me." He cleared his throat, then gave her a sheepish smile. "You are a lovely woman and a gracious host. I only hope we may begin again. My wife would be so pleased to be able to continue this friendship."

His speech took her by surprise. Her cheeks warmed at his compliment, and she knew by the seriousness in his dark eyes that he was sincere. She grasped his hand and gave him a smile. "I would like that very much, Lord Elwood. Very much."

"Elwood, dear," came his wife's voice from a distance. "Where did you go off to?"

"My dearest calls," he said with a lopsided smile. "Thank you, Lady Winfield."

Christiana sat down in front of the hearth, letting her mind wander over the past few days. She leaned her head against the soft leather of the wingback chair, comparing her opinion of her guests when they first arrived with her present thoughts. How wrong she had been about them. Well, most of them. Lord Frederick was still a toad and probably always would be.

Lord Elwood was a different man with Lady Elwood by his side. His pompous attitude had been a show of bravado. In truth, he was a kind man who loved his wife and enjoyed hunting. And Lady Elwood had indeed become a friend. They had spent the early afternoons conversing over needlepoint and the evenings laughing and discussing fashion, men, books, and life. The viscountess was a wonderful listener with a natural maternal instinct, and Christiana found herself wanting to confide in the woman.

Lord Bentson, the dear man, had shared several stories

about her mother. How wonderful it was to learn a new side of Mama, told by someone who had loved her. He had asked if he could continue to write, and Christiana had agreed. She was growing attached to the elderly man and had even caught herself slapping her knee once.

"What deep thoughts are swirling in that beautiful brain of yours?"

She turned to see Lucius leaning against the doorframe. "Thinking of first impressions and how wrong it can be not to keep an open mind."

"As in the Elwoods?" he asked, taking the seat next to her.

She nodded. "And Lord Bentson."

"Has he told you more about his time with your mother?"

Again, she nodded, thinking how handsome he looked in his mulberry coat and black and white pinstriped waistcoat. His hair was combed back, curling around his nape. "He's a sweet man. I'm growing quite fond of him."

"I've enjoyed their company as well. Lord Bentson is full of surprises. Who would guess a man of his age could still manage a bow and a pistol with such skill?"

"It makes me wonder what other tricks he hasn't revealed yet."

"Who do you think will win?"

"All of them." Including herself. For she would win Lucius. Maybe it was time to stop denying her feelings, face her fears, and admit she wanted to be with Lord Page. Did she want to be Lady Page and part of his obnoxious, loving family? Be a sister to Lady Annette and a mother to an entire brood of rambunctious, ornery boys just like the Page brothers? Perhaps she did.

Christiana gave him a side-look and grinned at his shocked expression.

"How can they all win?" Lucius rested one ankle on the

opposite knee, leaning his head back. "Do you anticipate a three-way tie?"

"No." She laughed, and once again, the familiar light-hearted feeling returned. "Believe it or not, I have made friends during this house party. I like them, and dealing with them as friends rather than business acquaintances seems like a victory for me."

"So, you will sell everything except Vengeance?"

"No, I will sell the vase and will allow Lord Elwood and his guests access to my woods." She imagined the smiles on the Elwoods when they learned of her decision. "They will have to notify me, of course, which will provide us with future opportunities to enjoy one another's company."

"Clever. What about the mines Sir Horace wants to buy?"

She flashed him a sly smile. "I'm still considering what to do about that."

"Ah, then everyone may not win."

"I must keep someone on his toes." Christiana stood. "Midnight?"

He shook his head. "I'm exhausted. If I wait until then, I'll fall asleep."

"Shall we wait until tomorrow?" She bit her lip, not wanting him to see her disappointment.

"Egad, no. And miss my bedtime kiss? Your lips give me the most delicious dreams. Without it, I fear I might have nightmares." He rose and stood before her, arms behind his back. "Get your cloak and meet me outside. I have a different version of this afternoon's contest."

Christiana dismissed Mr. Jensen before she joined Lucius, assuring the butler that she would be perfectly safe. From his quick assent, she knew he was beginning to trust Lord Page. The night sky had cleared to an inky black with a bright moon guiding her way along the path.

"I only brought two pistols," said Lucius when she stood next to him.

"So, how is this contest different?" A kiss between each shot? She would agree to it, she thought with a grin.

"Only one shot and there will be diversions. We are allowed to do anything to distract one another *except* use our hands." His green eyes smoldered when he said *anything*. But without touching? Interesting.

Christiana picked up her pistol and took her mark. A new wafer was tacked to the same tree. As she gripped the handle and held out her arm, his warm breath caressed her cheek. Her stomach tumbled.

"So this is how it's going to be?" she asked.

"Indeed," he whispered in her ear.

Once again, she took aim, and just as she squeezed the trigger, Lucius nibbled at her earlobe. The gun went off. She barely made the wafer yet found she wasn't at all disappointed. For now, it was her turn.

Lucius took her place. Christiana fetched both pistol cases, stacked them on the ground, and used them as a step. Now she could reach above his shoulders. When he raised his arm, she tucked her nose under his thick brown curls and brushed her lips across his nape.

"I knew this was a good idea," his voice low, husky.

He raised his arm again, and she trailed kisses across his jaw. When he pulled the trigger, she whispered in his ear, "I want you." He froze, pistol still aimed at the wafer on the tree, jaw tense, his mouth a grim line. But the shot was dead center.

She had just given herself to him, and he seemed ready to explode. "Are you angry?"

***

Lucius couldn't move. *I want you.* Not love, but want. He

needed to make her understand there was no compromising on the issue of wedlock.

"I think you should know," he said, studying her expression as he continued, "I decided this was the last year I would send you a token. It is time I marry, begin my own family, and produce a future heir."

She blinked, her long blonde lashes covering the disappointment in her sky-blue eyes. The corners of her mouth tipped down slightly. *Good, let her see my urgency.*

"Then my brother arrived with his friend, holding an invitation, the key to my heart. I thought fate was sending me one last chance. I took it and ran, in the hope that the future —our future—might still be attainable." He barked a hoarse laugh. "The golden ring, always just beyond my grasp." He reached out, took an amber lock between his fingers, wishing he wasn't wearing his gloves.

"You've always been a romantic," she said, but a smile curved her lips now. "I loved that about you."

His head jerked up at the word he'd been waiting to hear. Loved. As in the past? "And now? Do you still love that about me?"

She nodded, and her gloved fingers came up to touch his mouth, traced the creases framing each side. "And more." Her lips followed her fingers, caressing, softly pulling, then coaxed them to open for her.

Heat roared through his body, pulsing low and erratically as he crushed her body to his, her curves fitting perfectly with his lean, hard length. She was heaven, what his mind and body yearned for to be complete. His hands slipped beneath her mantle, lingered on her hips, and she moved against him, stoking the fire inside him into an inferno. Heaven and hell, want and need, all battling desire and uncertainty, all fighting to win this tug of war.

Lucius lost his reserve and peppered kisses at her temple,

along her cheek, down her jaw. Her head fell back, exposing the creamy skin of her long, slender neck. He was a man starved, a man held at bay too long, untying her cloak to expose her neck and holding the cape around her with one arm. He nipped and licked his way to her collarbone, kissed the line of her cleavage, then returned to her mouth. Her sweet, soft, tempting mouth. She shuddered beneath his hands.

"Say you love me. Not want, but *love*," he rasped in her ear. "I need to hear you say it, even if you turn me away in the end. Tell me I didn't waste all those years wondering, longing to see you, hold you, taste you."

Christiana shook her head. "I love you, Lucius Page, but I don't know if I'm ready to face life again on your terms." Her breath warmed his own neck as she spoke against it. "Convince me."

This time when their mouths clashed, it was Christiana who demanded, and Lucius gave in. He would do anything in his power to prove they were meant to be together, turn back time if he could.

Turn back time.

He smiled against her lips, the wheels already cranking to life as an idea began to form.

CHAPTER 13

29 December

*C*hristiana called everyone to attention. "Today we shall play croquet."

Lady Elwood pursed her lips. "But you said both of us could play, and it's cold outside." The viscountess brushed crumbs off her azure bodice, then finished her tea. "I'll stay here and finish the biscuits."

"It shall be an inside game."

All four sets of eyes locked on her.

"Croquet inside?" asked Lord Bentson.

"How will you get the hoops to stand?" asked Lord Elwood.

"Oh, I have no doubt she has a plan," said Lucius.

"When I was young," began Christiana, "my parents would make up inside games when the weather was bad. We would put numbers on pieces of furniture, and they would be our hoops. We would play from one room to the next and then move to the lower level."

Lord Bentson slapped his knee, his face crinkling with pleasure. "'Pon my soul, child, that is clever. I bet your mother thought it up."

Christiana smiled at him and nodded. "We will begin on the first floor in the small parlor and work our way back here. My lady's maid has placed the numbers on the next floor and will have them laid out down here when we return."

The group followed her upstairs, and each took a mallet with a ball. The upstairs parlor had a small hearth flanked by two small brocade chairs, a chaise longue by the window, and several tables.

"As you see, the paper on each piece of furniture tells you what order to send the ball." They took turns hitting the balls first under the chairs, then a side table, the length of the chaise longue, and under another table.

"Now what?" asked Lord Bentson, swinging his mallet like a dandy with a new cane.

Christiana walked to the top of the staircase and pointed at the bottom. A chair had been placed between the bottom step and the front door. "The ball must go down the stairs and under the chair. Then once we are back in the entryway, you must send the ball back under the chair and into the drawing room."

The chaos began. Lord Elwood sent his ball bouncing down the steps, on top of the chair, clunking against the front door. Lady Elwood's ball made it halfway down the steps and stopped. Lord Bentson got his ball to the bottom step but not beneath the chair. Lord Page managed to get his ball down the steps and under the chair.

Once in the entryway, Lord Elwood sent his ball back

under the chair, slamming Lord Page's ball toward the drawing room, and stopping below the last step. Lady Elwood tapped hers from the middle of the stairway, hit Lord Bentson's, which hit Lord Elwood's, and all three balls rolled in three different directions. The clank of wood and the exclamations and shouts from the players had Christiana laughing so hard, she had to wipe away tears.

"I do believe this is more fun as an adult," she said between hiccups. Lucius angled his ball from the drawing-room door to the center of the room. By the time Lucius was declared the winner, Lord Elwood had finally made it out of the entryway.

"Brandy is always a good idea after a battle," said Lord Bentson.

"I second that." Lord Elwood went to the side table and poured two glasses, then looked over his shoulder at Lord Page, who nodded. "Ladies? A drink? Some sherry?"

He passed out the drinks, and they settled back into the seats they'd claimed as their own during the house party. The atmosphere was jovial, and Christiana wanted the cama- raderie to continue.

"Lord Page has three points. He wins and will be granted the mines in Wales." Lord Bentson was the first to point out the obvious. "Although I'm disappointed, I have to say this is the best house party I've attended in years. And at my age, that's quite a list."

"I'm not actually gaining the mines. It's Sir Horace who is buying them," reminded Lucius.

Lady Elwood patted her husband's arm. "I'm sorry you didn't win, love."

"I admit I'm a bit disappointed, but I'm overjoyed you— we—have made a new friend. And to think she's been our neighbor all this time." He smiled down at his wife, then at

Christiana. "Lady Winfield, we hope to see much more of you in the coming months. My wife throws splendid garden parties. Or so I'm told."

Christiana beamed. "I have an announcement. This entire charade began to rid myself of all the men who wanted something from me. I thought I wanted peace and to be left alone. Instead, I have made new friends who I hope become dear old friends."

"A toast!" said Lucius, standing. "To a new year and new beginnings."

They held up their glasses and drank to one another.

"Lord Bentson, I am still willing to sell you the Ming vase. I believe my mother would have wanted you to have it." She smiled at him, her chest expanding with happiness. "However, your last offer was much too high. We shall come to a fair price before you leave."

"Lady Winfield, you are a diamond of the first water," he said, slapping his knee. "I thank you."

"Under one condition," she said. "We must keep in touch. I would be heartbroken if our time together ended here."

"I'd be honored. I have more stories to tell you," he agreed, his hazel eyes glistening.

"Lord Elwood, if we are to be *friends* as well as neighbors, I see no reason you cannot hunt on my property. My only request is you notify me, so I avoid that area when you are shooting." She grinned. "By notifying me, I mean an invitation to your lovely home which I would love to visit."

"Oh my dear, I can't stand it," cried Lady Elwood. She jumped from her chair and pulled Christiana from her seat, wrapping her in a fierce hug. "I've been wanting to do that for two days."

Christiana blinked back tears and soaked up all the kindness in the older woman's hug. All these years, she had lived in this huge house practically alone. Yet, these amazing people she had considered pests had been here all along. Waiting to befriend her.

***

Christiana descended the steps, wondering why Lucius had told her to dress in her favorite gown. Feeling sentimental, she wore the same gold silk skirt and bodice that had been packed away since the last time she'd danced with Lucius. The silver thread knotted along the square neckline and hem shimmered with each step. Constance had done her hair, a loose knot with silver ribbon woven into the chignon and long curls falling over her shoulders.

Lucius stepped out from beneath the staircase as she landed on the bottom step and held out his arm. "Lady Christiana, may I escort you to the ball?"

"What?" His grin was infectious, so she nodded, playing along when he addressed her as if she were not married. "Why yes, Lord Page, I'd be delighted."

They entered the drawing room, and she gasped at the dozens of candles casting a dazzling light about the room. The furniture had been pushed back to clear the center for dancing. Near the pianoforte sat Lord Bentson in a black evening coat and waistcoat, his cravat perfectly tied and pristine white. He bowed, picked up a violin, and the first notes of a waltz began.

Lord and Lady Elwood stepped from behind them and began to dance. The viscount was also dressed to the nines, and Lady Elwood wore a lovely rose satin gown with tiny paste diamonds along the bodice. Her hair was piled on top of her head with a tiara resting on top that glittered as she moved.

Lucius stood above her, his spicy scent and deep timbre tickling her senses. "Lady Christiana, may I have this dance?"

Without a word, she stepped into his arms. His hand was

warm and firm on her back, their palms together, holding her balanced as they turned. "You are an excellent dancer, Lord Page."

"I have an excellent partner," he said.

He made small talk as they waltzed, and some of it seemed familiar. He spoke of people they once knew, walks in Hyde Park, a soiree they had attended before she had married. After the dance, Lucius walked her to a side table where he poured her a drink from a punch bowl and offered her thin cucumber sandwiches.

"I feel like I'm back at Almack's," she said with a chuckle.

"Lud, I'd hate to be that young again," said Lady Elwood, then grunted when her husband poked her with his elbow. "We're happy you could attend our ball, Lord Page, Lady Christiana. Please enjoy yourselves."

The couple walked away, and Christiana frowned. Were they pretending to be someone else? She squinted at Lord Bentson across the room. He winked at her and picked his violin up again, beginning a second waltz.

"Let's shock the wagging tongues of London and dance a second time," Lucius said, taking her in his arms. When they neared the doorway, he twirled her into the entryway and out the front door, held open by Mr. Jensen.

"Lord Page, what are you doing?" she asked as the cold air sent goose bumps up her arms. Lucius took off his coat and put it around her shoulders.

"Lady Christiana, it is Christmastide, and my grand-mother always told me that anything is possible this time of year. In the spirit of this magical holiday, I have been granted the ability to turn the clock back for one night." He wrapped his arms about her and pulled her close. "So, I've returned us to the evening where everything might have been different."

Her heart pounded; her mouth went dry. "A second chance?"

He nodded, then bent his head, and kissed her. Her mind went back to the night she regretted with all her heart. She had been so confused, Edward so certain, and Lucius so desperate. If she had only known then...

His mouth claimed hers now, bringing her back again to the present. His urgency sent a lightning bolt of desire through her. His hands grasped her hips, pulling her against his hard length, then caressed her back.

Christiana wrapped her arms around his waist, the warmth of his shoulders seeping through his linen shirt and waistcoat. Her hands moved over him, feeling the muscles bunch under her touch, her lips seeking, wanting to prove her desire was as strong as his. She kissed him with all the pent-up longing of wasted years, the impatience of a woman starved.

When he ended the kiss, both of them panting despite the frigid temperatures, he said, "Lady Christiana, I beg of you. Marry me. The gossip will die down soon enough if you break off your engagement. Let us elope, go to Scotland tonight." He kissed her again, one hand cupping her jaw, his thumb stroking her cheek and catching her first tear.

"Make me the happiest of men and forsake your betrothed. I love you with a fierceness that I cannot tame. Marry me, Christiana. Right the wrongs of our past." His green eyes, dark with passion, locked with hers, his square jaw tense. "Let us not make the same mistake twice."

He was allowing her to toss her regret aside and choose again. But this time, her heart would make the right decision. "Yes, Lucius, yes. I will marry you. I will be your wife."

"Say it. Say the words, Christiana," he whispered in her ear.

"I love you, Lucius Page. I love you with all my heart."

"I want you to repeat those words every day for the rest of our lives."

From the door, the clapping and cheering commenced. Lord and Lady Elwood let out whoops of joy, Lord Bentson began a lively tune on the violin, and Mr. Jensen held the door open to welcome them back to the present time.

"Get out of the cold, you young fools," cried Lady Elwood. "Celebrate in front of the Yule log."

EPILOGUE

November 1821

Lucius held out the box with a grin. "Another year of beauty gained."

Christiana took the box and laughed. "Tell me that in twenty years."

Life had changed so much since last November. Marriage with Lucius had been everything he had promised. Love, family, friends. They had decided to live at Falcon Hall, giving Lucius's father and his new wife privacy. The Elwoods were frequent dinner companions, and Lord Elwood had recently presented her with venison, courtesy of his last hunt.

Lord Bentson would be their guest for Christmastide again. She was already planning the house party for this year, hoping Lucius's sister, Annette, and her husband, Lord Weston, would join them.

Christiana untied the ribbon and lifted the lid of the box.

"Oh, Lucius, it's beautiful." She lifted the crystal dove from its nest of velvet and held it up to the light.

"Just as you are. It's a symbol of our love and the peace you have brought to my soul by becoming my wife."

"You have given me the same." She stretched on her tiptoes and kissed his cheek.

He shook his head and pulled her close. "That won't do." His lips covered hers, not stopping their sweet assault until she was breathless.

"The aviary will be finished next spring. Would you like a pair of doves for it?"

She blinked back tears. Tears of joy for a year of bliss, with more blessings coming in the next year. "My heart is already so full."

"I'll stretch it to make room for I have decades more to spoil you, my sweet bird," he said and kissed her again.

"I have something for you too," she said.

"It's not my day," he objected. "I have my heart's desire right here."

"Consider it an early Christmas present. For if I wait, you might guess before that day arrives." She carefully placed the dove in the curio cabinet, then walked to the big oak desk. Pulling a small velvet bag from the top drawer, she handed it to Lucius.

He gave her an odd look, then opened the bag, and shook out the contents. A delicately carved bird of white ivory lay in his palm. His brows drew together, then his eyes widened. "A stork?"

"A symbol of life," she said, beaming.

"A baby?" he asked. "We're having a baby?"

He picked her up and twirled her around and around. Christiana laughed and let her head drop back, enjoying the spinning sensation and the joy radiating off her husband.

The library banged open, a hulking Mr. Jensen darkening

the doorway, a scowl on his face. Lucius stopped turning and let Christiana slide to the carpet. "He really needs to get out of that habit," mumbled Lucius, scowling back at the butler.

"We're fine, Mr. Jensen."

"I'm going to be a father," yelled Lucius, picking Christiana up again and spinning her in the opposite direction. "You shall be an uncle, Jensen."

The butler stared at them, and slowly, very slowly, a grin stretched across his face. He let out a howl that would frighten a banshee.

Christiana laughed, wrapping her arms around her husband's neck. She thought of the little sparrow, so easily lost in a gale. She had been lost, afraid to find her way. Lucius had broken through the storm and brought her back. He would always be her sun, breaking through the clouds to guide her home.

REVIEWS ARE the lifeblood of an author. If you enjoyed this story, please consider leaving a few words on your favorite retailer's site.

IF YOU WERE INTRIGUED by Lucius's sister, read about Lady Annette and Lord Weston in *A Wallflower's Wassail Punch*.

ABOUT THE AUTHOR

USA Today Bestselling author Aubrey Wynne resides in the Midwest with her husband, dogs, horses, mule, and barn cats. Obsessions include wine, history, travel, trail riding, and all things Christmas. Her Chicago Christmas series and historical romances have received multiple awards and nominations as a Rone finalist by InD'tale Magazine.

Aubrey's first love is medieval romance but after dipping her toe in the Regency period in 2018 with the *Wicked Earls' Club*, she was smitten. This inspired her sweet Regency spin-off series *Once Upon a Widow*, and a steamy Scottish Regency series, *A MacNaughton Castle Romance*. Her Regency detective series, *Paddy's Peelers*, will launch in 2025.

Social Media Links:
Website:
http://www.aubreywynne.com
Facebook:
https://www.facebook.com/magnificentvalor
Aubrey's Ever After Facebook group:
https://www.facebook.com/groups/AubreyWynnesEverAfters/
Twitter:
https://twitter.com/Aubreywynne51
Pinterest:
https://www.pinterest.com/aubreywynne51/

Instagram:

https://www.instagram.com/Aubreywynne51

Bookbub page:

https://www.bookbub.com/profile/aubrey-wynne

Goodreads:

https://www.goodreads.com/author/show/7383937.Aubrey_Wynne

Sign up for my newsletter and don't miss future releases

https://www.subscribepage.com/k3f1z5

ALSO BY AUBREY WYNNE

Once Upon a Widow series

Earl of Sunderland #1

Maggie award, International Digital Awards finalist

Christopher Roker inherited the title of rake. She hides behind her independence. Fate accepts the challenge...

Escaping his late brother's memory, Lady Grace is a welcome distraction. But as the attraction grows, Kit finds himself wavering between his old military life and the lure of an exceptional but unwilling woman.

A Wicked Earl's Widow #2

Recommended by InD'tale Magazine

Eliza, Lady Sunderland, is widowed after one year. Her abusive father, near financial ruin, is already planning another wedding.

When Viscount Pendleton discovers a beauty defending an elderly woman against ruffians, he is smitten. But Nate soon realizes he must discover Eliza's dark past to save the woman he loves.

Rhapsody and Rebellion #3

Maggie finalist, nominated for Rone Award, InD'tale Magazine

A Scottish legacy... A political rebellion... Two hearts destined to meet...

Alisabeth was betrothed from the cradle. At seventeen, she marries her best friend and finds happiness if not passion. In less than a year, a political rebellion makes her a widow. The handsome English earl arrives a month later and rouses her desire and a terrible guilt.

Crossing the border into Scotland, Gideon finds his predictable world turned upside down. Folklore, legend, and political unrest intertwine with an unexpected attraction to a feisty Highland beauty. When the earl learns of an English plot to stir the Scots into rebellion, he must choose his country or save the clan and the woman who stirs his soul.

Earl of Darby #4

Holt Medallion Winner, NTRWA Reader's Choice Award, Nominated for Rone Award, InD'tale magazine

Miss Hannah Pendleton, nursing her pride after her childhood crush falls in love with another, hurls herself into the excitement of a first season.

Since his wife's suicide on their wedding night, the Earl of Darby has carefully cultivated his rakish reputation. But when Nicholas sees a lovely newcomer being courted by the devil himself, her innocence and candor revive the chivalry buried deep in his soul.

Earl of Brecken #5

He's on the brink of ruin. She's in search of a hero.

Notorious for his seductive charm, the Earl of Brecken searches for a wealthy heiress. His choices are dismal until he meets Miss Franklin. Guileless, gorgeous and with an enormous dowry, she seems the answer to his prayers. Until his conscience makes an unexpected appearance.

Earl of Griffith #6

Sorrow and Regrets...

After eloping, a widowed Lady Helen is disillusioned with love and raising a three-year-old alone. Now she must face the music and her family.

An unexpected ray of sunshine...

Conway, Earl of Griffith is smitten at first sight with his friend's sister and adorable daughter. But can he convince the grieving and lovely widow that love is worth a second chance?

Beware A Wallflower's Wrath #7

Annis Craigg gave her heart—and innocence—away at seventeen. When Lord Robert Harding returns to Scotland fifteen years later, he's desperate to find the only woman he's ever loved. But she has secrets and an attitude.

Lies, secrets, and betrayal will challenge the fierce love of a steadfast Highlander and remorseful but determined Englishman. Will destiny find a way to bring two star-crossed souls together?

A Wallflower's Wassail Punch #8

Lady Annette's first Season was a disaster after a duke's son pinched her by the punchbowl, and she walloped him in the nose. Five years of malicious rumors later, her father offers an outrageous dowry so he too can marry.

Lord Wilkinson, a widower, meets a striking, intelligent woman, with a dry wit only he seems to appreciate. His heart stirs for the first time in decades. But will their age difference and wagging tongues interfere with their budding romance?

The Scoundrel's Christmas Challenge #9

A contest to win her fortune...

Lady Winfield, a long-time wealthy widow, is infamous for her outrageous house parties. While hosting her annual Christmastide gathering, Christiana proposes a new game: a daily challenge of her choice. She will accept the proposal of the man who can best her at three or more competitions by Twelfth Night. Though all agree to the diversion, no one expects the games to include marksmanship, archery, and fencing.

A contest to win her heart...

When Lucius, Viscount Bolingbroke presents Lady Winfield with a secret challenge, she can't resist. Will their midnight rendezvous and private contests end in certain victory for one or a dual attraction for both?

The Duplicate Duke #10

In a country far, far away...

Lady Gwendolyn Beaumaris and her brother have been known as the Downing twins since their father's death when they were eight years old. At twenty-two, Gwen and her mother have settled in Boston while her brother tries to make his fortune in the fur trade. Down to their last pennies, she must consider marriage to a wealthy middle-aged merchant.

The brass ring is so close...

Lord Wickton has worked tirelessly the past two years to bring honor back to the family name. When the viscount learns he is the heir presumptive to his great uncle's dukedom, his prayers are answered.

A comedy of errors...

When a letter arrives announcing that Gwen's brother is the new Duke of Shackerley, mother and daughter come up with a desperate plan: Gwendolyn will impersonate her brother and assume the dukedom. But when the sinfully handsome Wickton meets them at the dock, and Gwen is hopelessly smitten.

A tale of love, deception, and the power of fate will entangle a desperate viscount with a daring female. Can he forgive her charade, or will he snuff out the burning passion that rages in her heart.

A MacNaughton Castle Romance series

Highland Regencies

"Witty and sensual!"

Verified Purchase Review

"Lovely characters and complicated family conflicts. You will easily get caught up in their lives."

Goodreads Review

A Merry MacNaughton Mishap (Prequel)

Rone finalist, InD'tale Magazine, N.N. Light Book Heaven finalist

Two feuding clans, one accidental encounter, a wee bit of holiday enchantment…

When Calum MacNaughton rescues a rival clan member from an icy drowning, he is unexpectedly rewarded with the clansman's most precious possession. Now Calum has until Twelfth Night to convince her to stay.

Deception and Desire #1

Nominated for Rone award, InD'tale Magazine, N.N. Light Book Heaven award winner

Two rebellious souls… An innocent deception… One scorching catastrophe…

Fenella Franklin's talents lie in numbers and a keen business mind, not in the art of flirtation. Lachlan MacNaughton has neither the temperament nor the patience to be the next MacNaughton chief, preferring to knock heads together rather than placate bickering clansmen. Their attraction sparks a passion they cannot deny. But will an innocent deception test their newfound love?

Allusive Love #2

A woman in love… An infuriating Scot… A tantalizing chase.

Kirstine has loved Brodie MacNaughton forever, but he considers Kirsty his best friend. When he turns to her for advice, she surprises him with an unexpected kiss that sends fire through his veins. When pride, Highland politics, and tragedy collide, he realizes how precious and allusive true love can be.

A Bonny Pretender #3

She's pretending to be someone she's not… His entire life is based on a lie…

Brigid MacNaughton becomes the perfect lady to placate her family, then falls in love with a quiet, self-possessed Englishman. Lord Raines is smitten with the beguiling and demure Scot. If he divulges his scandalous parentage, will she still fall willingly into his arms? Bonny pretender vs handsome imposter… Can love overcome a double deception?

A Medieval Encounter Series

Rolf's Quest

Great Expectations winner, Fire & Ice, Maggie finalist

"Romance, destiny, family values & betrayal all played parts in this intriguing novel that had me turning each page in anticipation."

The BookTweeter

A wizard, a curse, a fated love...

When Rolf finally discovers the woman who can end the curse that has plagued his family for centuries, she is already betrothed. Time is running out for the royal wizard of King Henry II. If he cannot find true love without the use of sorcery, the magic will die for future generations.

Melissa is intrigued by the mystical, handsome man who haunts her by night and tempts her by day. His bizarre tale of Merlin, enchantments, and finding genuine love has her questioning his sanity and her heart.

From the moment Melissa stepped from his dreams and into his arms, Rolf knew she was his destiny. Now, he will battle against time, a powerful duke, and call on the gods to save her.

Saving Grace (A Small Town Romance)

Contemporary and Colonial America

Holt and Maggie finalist

This unique piece has the reader traveling between the early 1700s and the early 2000s with ease and amazement. The audience truly feels sorrow for Grace and Chloe and is able to connect with each woman for the hardships they are overcoming... The attention to historical facts and details leave one breathless, especially upon learning the people from the past did exist and the memorial erected still stands.

InD'tale Magazine

A tortured soul meets a shattered heart...

Chloe Hicks' life consisted of an egocentric ex-husband, a pile of bills, and an equine business in foreclosure until a fire destroys the stable and her beloved ranch horse. After the marshal suspects arson, she escapes the accusing eyes of her hometown.

Jackson Hahn, the local historian, distracts Chloe with a 17th-century legend of a woman wrongly accused of witchcraft. It might explain the ghostly happenings on the property. She is drawn to the similarities that plagued both their lives. Perhaps the past can help heal the present. But danger lurks in the shadows...